"Fillippi is more t[...] sar. It's not only a [...] nest of slave-holder[...] keeps reminding us. [...] lippi are anything bu[...] say the degenerate Co[...]ey run the place. . . . They pay the taxes— they can afford to. And their troops arrive on Riondi in good order. They're full of Menoma, of course, but our military people don't seem to mind that."

"Menoma?" Mart asked. "What is it? A drug?"

"Curious little stuff, Menoma. Interferes with the memory. You take it and you don't remember. For instance, you don't re- member you're Commissar Frederick, a man condemned to die. You don't remem- ber how to walk, either, but there are ways to fix that. . . ."

Mart understood vaguely. "What precisely have you got in mind?"

"We want you to go in there and topple the Concession. Very simple really. If you de- liver Fillippi, we give you a ticket to the nearest Empire planet. Your alternative is jail—forever."

The Siege of Faltara

Arsen Darnay

ace books

A Division of Charter Communications Inc.
A GROSSET & DUNLAP COMPANY
360 Park Avenue South
New York, New York 10010

THE SIEGE OF FALTARA

Copyright © 1978 by Arsen Darnay

An ACE Book

Cover art by Boris

First Ace printing: November 1978

Printed in U.S.A.

CONTENTS

PROLOGUE:
INTRODUCTION TO
OUTERMOST

Few of our publications have enjoyed the popularity of that enchanting series all of you know as *Sagas from New Frontier*. We have brought you, over a number of years, stories placed in a New Frontier setting, helping you back home to see and feel what life was like for the hardy pioneers who explored the countless worlds of our galaxy's X-Quadrant region.

But while we enjoyed bringing you *Sagas*, exploration has continued apace, and now for a number of decades a new story has been in the making: the conquest of Outermost. As you well know from watching the news, New Frontier is no longer what it used to be—certainly not the exciting quadrant it was when *Sagas* was initially started. The publishing world must keep up with the times. Thus, with great regret, we hereby announce the termination of the New Frontier series.

All things must end, but we have something else to replace your favorite entertainment reading. Permanent linkages have been established recently with the Milky Way's dexter spiral arm known to all as Outermost. Now we can communicate with that faraway region—and travel there directly—using several newly established time-collapse channels. And for the first time in many years, we are in a position to offer you something else: *Tales from Outermost!*

Whether *Tales* shall be as popular as *Sagas*, only you, the readers, can tell. We certainly hope you shall, and to test your inclinations, we herewith present The Siege of Faltara.

Outermost is composed of fifty thousand inhabited planets in nearly as many solar systems in our dexter spiral arm. Politically there are three camps. *Commercial System* controls ten thousand planets, *Empire* has the loyalty of roughly the same number. The remaining thirty thousand worlds are uncommitted to either side and under local rule. Not surprisingly, both System and Empire are doing their utmost to win the hearts of the people on the uncommitted planets; as you might guess, there is a good deal of conflict and adventure as these superpowers clash.

Outermost . . . It's still a wild galactic region. To most of you it would seem delightfully empty, beautiful, exhilarating, dangerous, and rich with unpredictability. None of our wise policies of social mass control are practiced. They still fight wars and breed freely rather than by compatibility matrix. Unbalanced personalities sometimes hold power—there is cruelty and ambition, intrigue and assassination . . . but also an engaging naivete, idealism, and innocence. Some worlds are paradisical. On the other hand, ecological disasters are a commonplace. The heady fumes of religion waft over those star-lit spaces. No one in Outermost has found the Way of Coexistence. Out there mankind still dreams childish dreams.

Our story is based on Fillippi, a water-planet of the System federation. Faltara is one of Fillippi's largest islands. In the grand scheme of galactic history, this episode hardly matters. Many more and grander tales will follow. But the story of the Fillippi Concession and of the Cush revolt will serve to introduce you to Outermost. On the planet of Fillippi, you will meet the first people of that region ever to play their roles before your eyes. You will learn of practices long forgotten—and long forbidden—in more settled areas. You will get a flavor of life in Outermost, its people, its mores. And who knows. Some of you might like Outermost well enough to go there and see for yourselves! A free passage to Outermost is now available courtesy of the Department of Population under the provisions of the Pressure Release Act. There is no cost to you. In fact, you will receive a generous stake to get you started. You are free to go and *live* the adventures that, at home, you can only read about.

As in *Sagas from New Frontier,* so in this story, what you read will be the truth. It comes to you in the tradition of strict realism for which this Office is justly famous. It is based on documentary evidence provided by System's Ministry of Development and Empire's Party Subplenum for Expansion. The story has been retold in the form of a tale—but merely for your greater enjoyment.

We hope that you will enjoy the Siege of Faltara. Should you wish to know more about Outermost, this story, emigration programs offered by the Department of Population, or any other related matter, please send your time-collapse information request to:

> The Editors
> Public Affairs Office
> Social Mass Control Branch
> Rim World Programs
> Department of Population
> Sol/Earth
> TC Code 56577898

PART I

THE CHALLENGE

1 — THE FOMPUS

According to a persistent rumor, Balto Fangano has challenged Butter Ball. "Balto Fangano?" you ask. We are as astonished as you are, but a little research has revealed a minor family by that name sporting as its emblem the "platypus," no less. Imagine the platypus battling felina! The Fanganos have never been linked with politics before—or anything else. If this rumor is true, the Faltara Games will be quite an event this year. Do you realize that "Seven Lives" has not been challenged in three years? And never to a tafpa joust?
>   —*From* Looking Glass, *the underground*
>   *newsletter of the Fillipi*
>   *Concession*

Dominus, the levitating city, floated at cloud level over the measureless oceans of Fillippi. Trade winds moved it slowly to the east, but the Island of Faltara, the city's next point of anchorage, was still five days away. Nonetheless, busy preparations for the so-called "Siege of Faltara" were underway in every palace up on Dominus. Slaves readied gear for the descent, lords and ladies selected wardrobes, fompa and guard officers put finishing touches on entertainment and security plans, and the administrative apparatus worked day and night to prepare the airborne city for the tricky anchoring maneuvers off the Faltara shores.

The seldom-seen coordinator of all this activity

3

worked deep inside the largest palace of Dominus, the palace of the Contortus family, a massive complex of stone with many towers.

He was Farnit Drusilla, chief fompus of the Contortus household. As stewart and general administrator of the family, he was a very important personage. He ran the family; and the family ran the planet's security forces; and hence, as Drusilla sometimes observed with unsmiling pleasure, he was the real master of Fillippi—even if the titular role fell on the overfat and hapless shoulders of Ignazio Contortus, the boy-general of the tundrati.

Drusilla was a tall, thin, unsmiling, ascetic man who shaved his head until it shone like a mirror. Today, as always, he was dressed in a simple silver robe. He sat in a small, windowless cubicle of an office whose walls were painted a cheerless, almost an aggressive white. Charts on the wall, the communications gear on tables, the papers on his desk—all of these objects were arranged with great precision and breathed an almost vengeful air of order.

Drusilla sat behind the desk inspecting the morning's mail. One of his subordinates sat opposite, a writing tablet on his lap; he took down Drusilla's instructions. Like the chief fompus, Carlos also shaved his head; but he wore a simple blue robe to indicate his inferior rank.

As Drusilla shuffled papers, he came across a piece of smooth leather of blue coloration, a small section of tafpa hide. Words had been burned into the leather. It was a challenge.

He read the letter quickly, mumbling under his breath. "Balto Fangano . . . under the constitutional provisions . . . hereby exercises the right . . . challenge Ignazio . . . position of Controller of Tundrata . . ."

The fompus lifted his shiny head and tossed the leather to Carlos.

"Another challenge from some obscure family," he said. "Balto Fangano. Never heard of him."

"Must be one of the minor families," Carlos said.

"I expect so. *Very* minor. Look into it and find out what they *really* want."

Challenges like this one came routinely to the Contortus household. Under the constitutional amendments of 863, passed some ten years earlier with Drusilla's not too gentle support, the political duel had become the only legitimate form of succession on Fillippi. To get another person's job, you challenged him to combat. The person could yield the position, negotiate for a settlement, or gird himself to fight.

Many people challenged Ignazio Contortus never intending to do battle. They simply wanted attention from the powerful Contortus household—and usually some small privilege.

Drusilla guessed that the obscure Fangano family fell into this category. No doubt they wanted a little more land on one of the islands, an increase in slave allotments, or some other trifle.

He forgot the matter until the following day; then it surfaced again annoyingly. Carlos had called a member of the Fangano household and had learned that the Fanganos considered this a serious challenge. Incredibly, they refused to negotiate.

Drusilla frowned when he heard about this.

"Are they just stalling? Is this some kind of stratagem?"

Carlos lifted his shoulders.

"I can't waste time on this just now," Drusilla said.

He had his hands full. The rebellious underground—the Cush—had started troubles in the Illoppo

chain of islands again, and Drusilla oversaw the
military operations to wipe them out; some people in
the senate had begun to agitate again, their aim to
remove the duelling requirements of the constitution;
the anchoring maneuvers outside Faltara were difficult
owing to the diamond-hardness of the ocean floor.
Drusilla had many things to do.

"I can't follow up on this," he said. "Not until
we're anchored. But get some people on this. I want to
know all about these damn Fanganos. Everything. Get
back to me after you do some digging." The aide
turned to go, but Drusilla stopped him. "And by the
way. I want this treated as administratively secret. I
don't want any leaks. Above all, the family mustn't
learn about this."

Carlos nodded.

"Keep Sol Teck out of it too."

The aide nodded again.

"I don't want him running to Uncle Cullu—and he
will, by God, the moment he hears of this."

Carlos grinned.

"It's no joking matter, Carlos," Drusilla said. Then
he waved a hand, dismissing the aide.

Drusilla stood behind his desk for a moment longer,
lost in thought. Three years had passed since Ignazio
had had to fight an actual duel. Sol Teck—who was
Drusilla's deputy in title but rival in fact—would make
the most of this occasion. Sol Teck was loyal to Lord
Cullu, Ignazio's uncle and head of the poorer side of the
family. So Teck would stir up Uncle Cullu and Cullu
would rouse the other members of the family. They
thirsted for a chance to slip out of Drusilla's iron
grip—but if they ever did, God save them, Drusilla
thought. This planet would eat them alive.

Drusilla's frown deepened. Fillippi was ruled by a

Concession, an aggregation of owners, of stockholders, fifty-some-odd families. Drusilla had made it a matter of policy to know all about the leading families—and some of the upstarts too. Now he blamed himself for his neglect of the Fanganos. It seemed to him he hadn't even heard the name before.

He shook his bald head slowly. Then, with an effort, he turned his considerable powers of concentration to other and more pressing matters.

Two days later Carlos reported on the fruits of his investigation, and Drusilla learned that the Fanganos were immigrants from New Frontier. Carlos described them as "typical escapees from civilization; they are rich adventurers." They had arrived on Fillippi four years earlier and had bought a share of the Concession after touchdown.

"Did you say *one* share?"

Carlos nodded. "One solitary share."

No wonder, Drusilla thought. A one-share family did not deserve attention—much less the investment of an agent or two to supervise them. Puzzling, very puzzling. The gall of these people. A one-share family should not presume to challenge *any* official of the Concession. To challenge Ignazio, general of the tundrati . . . it simply wasn't done.

"Could it be that they're naive?" he asked. "Could it be that they don't know the way the game is played around here?"

Carlos wriggled in discomfort. "The trouble is . . . You see, fompus, we can't get any really hard information. We can't get inside the household—and we've tried. But they are tight—tighter than a submarine. Their people won't take bribes. The chief fompus of the household is a strange sort—he just smiles. He said that

Balto has one objective. He wants to command the tundrati. And he insists that he has every right to challenge Ignazio.''

"Balto, you mean?"

"Yes."

"That he does," Drusilla said dryly. "What sort of a man is he, this Balto Fangano?"

"Big," Carlos said. "A huge bear of a man."

Drusilla frowned. He couldn't place Balto Fangano. "Anything else? Is there any more?"

"We have a detailed family history, of course. And photographs."

"No. I mean—did you find anything significant? A point of leverage?"

"They are advertising for a tafpa master. They are offering a salary of two hundred credits a week."

"*How* much?"

"Two hundred."

Drusilla shook his head. A handsome salary, handsome indeed. It should buy three tafpa masters. "And?" he asked. "What have we done about it?"

"I put the word out," Carlos said. "I put out word 'discouraging' any master from applying."

"Good."

"I've also found a man who might be right for the job. His name is Brudd, Captain Brudd. Some time ago he was a commander here, with the palace guard. He has some experience with tafpas."

"Isn't he the man we shipped off to Riondi? The fellow with the drinking problem?"

Carlos nodded.

"Can we get him released?"

"I checked with the System Military Authority. SMA says that it's all right with them—provided we replace him. I got the idea that Brudd is not exactly loved up there."

Drusilla pondered the matter. "I don't blame them. Brudd is not the most trustworthy of people . . ."

"I agree," Carlos said, "but there are very few people with tafpa training who are loyal to Concession—much less loyal to this household. I ran a computer search. Brudd is just about the best we can do."

"Well, then . . . Let's move on that," Drusilla said. He sat for a moment staring at the tidy desk. "A tafpa master," he said. Strange, very strange. The Fanganos were either very stupid or very subtle. "Well," he said, looking up at Carlos, "let's talk about details."

On the fifth day after the challenge had arrived, and soon after Dominus had been anchored off the coast of Faltara, Drusilla went to see his titular master. Lord Ignazio had to be told.

Ignazio was up in his secluded East Tower apartment—his favorite hiding place. The young lord was uncommonly fat, very shy, and pathologically fearful of assassination. He occupied himself with Menoma slaves; he watched entertainments on the time-collapse; and at times he played the martinet with a selected platoon of palace guards Drusilla had put at his disposal. Beyond these activities, Ignazio paid no attention to his job. Drusilla did the real work of commanding the tundrati. There were times, however, such as the present time, when even Ignazio had a need to know.

Ignazio stood behind a glass desk; he was leaning down, pudgy fists propped for support. He read and reread the challenge letter Drusilla had laid before him. When he moved, the diamonds on his shoulder-boards threw sun reflections around the circular tower room. In his bright red jacket, tan britches, and black boots, Ignazio was dressed for the parade ground. His hair, worn down to his shoulders, was bleached in the center to create a hairdo Fillippi's fashion called "the streak."

Drusilla stood opposite, arms folded across his chest. His shaven head reflected light and gave him an aura of single-minded purpose. Once more he wore a long silver robe. A wide black belt encircled his waist. Through open sandals could be seen the stumps of three toes on his left foot. A now dead Contortus lord had long ago ordered them sawed off with a table knife at a whim. That lord had died violently, and Drusilla had come a long ways since then. But the missing toes caused him to walk with a stiff and stilted gait—like Fillippi's long-legged, purple-and-white water bird, the mingo-linga.

Drusilla grew impatient. He glanced at the powdered Menoma slave-girls standing against the walls holding trays with snacks for Iggy's instant gratification. Their eyes were blank. Their faces, shoulders, breasts, and bellies had been powdered to kill the greenish tint skin took on under excessive Menoma dosage. These were so-called "intimates." They received nightly Menoma injections to help them forget whatever they had heard. In two or three months they would be dead. They were patient—like the walls. But Drusilla had things to do.

"Reading that letter over and over again, my lord," he said, "what's the use of that? The facts are simple. Fangano has challenged you to a tafpa joust. I don't know his motives—and the intelligence is sparse just now."

Ignazio looked up. His eyes peered out over small

ramparts of flesh with a worried expression. His full red lips trembled as he prepared to speak.

"I don't like it, Farnit. I don't like it at all."

"Who likes surprises?" the fompus said. "But face the facts, my lord. This is not your first challenge—nor likely to be your last. We have gained control of the Concession by facing up to such things."

"Balto Fangano, Balto Fangano," the young Contortus muttered. "Who are the Fanganos? What do we know about them?"

Drusilla sighed. "They are one of the minor families, my lord. They came here four years ago. They are dull and undistinguished people from Felicitas in New Frontier, a well-known heavy planet. They're big, stocky, and easygoing people—a trait that goes with heavy planets, I'm told. They dabble in science. And they like to eat. Balto claims to be a geologist. Most of the time he is down on one of the islands with a hammer and a little leather bag. He collects rocks. He claims that Fillippi had continents long ago. I suppose that a man from Felicitas can't quite believe in a water planet—not even when he lives on one. He fancies sunken continents everywhere."

Carlos had shown Drusilla a photograph of Balto—a big man with a square, smiling face dressed in dusty overalls and heavy boots. Like a peasant. He had had a loose and untidy look. Reflecting on that image, Drusilla went on.

"He is not a typical Castle-lord." Then he thought of another addition. "The family emblem is the platypus—the Felicitas variety."

Ignazio shook his head in a puzzled, agitated manner. Drusilla's reference to water planets had turned his attention to the globe on his desk—a blue ball with white polar caps and a string of small, brownish islands around the equator. The islands resembled a crude belt. In the northern hydrosphere Drusilla could see a faint S-shaped outline close to the north pole; it was the Illoppo chain, the scene of recent battles.

Ignazio peered at the fompus.

"Could this have some connection with Cush?"

"Cush?" Drusilla said, genuinely surprised. "I should say not, my lord. No family up here in Castle could conceivably be linked with Cush. Cush has one objective—to topple the Concession and to turn Fillippi into a republic; how could anyone up here benefit from that? The Fanganos use Menoma slaves like everyone else; why should they willingly expose themselves to System's justice? But let us assume that they are linked to Cush in some way—for the sake of argument. Cush has reached an all-time low at present; your victorious tundrati smashed four of their camps three weeks ago, and we think that we have sunk their miserable home-made submarine. Cush would make very poor allies for the Fanganos."

"Then this must be a genuine challenge," Ignazio cried. He hit the letter with his hand. His voice had taken on the shrill tone he used on the parade ground with his toy soldiers. "Balto wants to be commander! Why? I want to know why!"

Drusilla shrugged. He walked toward one of the oblong windows. One hand against the wall, he stared out. The sun blazed down on his bald, copper-red skull.

"Ambition? Eccentricity? Who knows, my lord. But I plan to find out. I have taken steps to penetrate the household. A captain from Riondi is on his way to be their tafpa master—which is no small coup for us. Soon we will know a good deal more."

Drusilla saw the ocean down below and a piece of Faltara. Dominus floated eight hundred meters above the waters, held aloft by a million liters of levitron. The tricky anchoring maneuver had cost a hundred thousand liters of the precious liquid. They had had to release lac to lower north corner so that the anchors would take hold.

He turned back to Ignazio. "I will report to you with any new information. Meanwhile, I suggest that you stop worrying. I will have a talk with Huroka so that the training can start right away. I will arrange for us to attend the tafpa auction at Potsla Run. We will buy the best animal they have. We have plenty of time to get ready. The games are still two months away."

Ignazio threw himself into a throne-like chair several sizes too big for him. He swivelled back and forth, a petulant look on his puffy face. "Why bother to buy a tafpa? Tafpa jousting is an art. Not even the best of beasts can help us."

"I'm not so sure," Drusilla said, but inwardly he shared Ignazio's apprehensions. He imagined how Huroka would react when told about his new assignment. The wrinkled little man would screw up his face and rasp out his objections without fear of rank. *What? Tafpa jousting? You must be kidding, Farnit. That's much too complex. We have tried that before, chief, remember? It was a mess. It can't be done—and don't you try to make me do it. Just tell blubber-boy to kiss it good-bye.* Well, Drusilla thought, Huroka would have to try it.

"I'm not so sure," he repeated. "Of course, I'll grant you this, my lord: I'd rather fight with pistols, choppers, speedboats—anything mechanical. We have tried all of those and we know that they work. But now we have to try tafpa jousting, and we might do very well."

Ignazio looked dubious.

"And even if things go wrong in training," Drusilla insisted, "the world will expect us to buy a top-rated jouster. We have to do it for show, if not for practical reasons."

"What about the family? Do they know?"

"Let me handle the family," Drusilla said. "I'll appreciate it if you don't receive Lord Cullu—or Sol Teck. To win this joust, I must have undisputed control over events."

"I haven't said that I'd accept the challenge."

"You must accept," Drusilla said. "You have no choice. You have to fight to keep your power. You have made too many enemies. Today the tundrati protect you. But if you give up your post, you'll be a constant target—of assassination, of more challenges. You mustn't weaken."

"I don't like it, Farnit. I don't like it at all."

Drusilla clicked his tongue impatiently. He had done his duty and had played the subordinate long enough. The time had come to break off this tiresome exchange.

"Pull yourself together, my lord," he said. "Take your mind off the matter. Your guard is waiting in the courtyard for the morning drill. And I have pressing business."

With that Drusilla bowed and left. His stilted gait recalled the mingo-linga stalking among the reeds.

He made for the main palace building by way of a roofed-over bridge with open sides. Halfway across, he paused to take in the view of Faltara eight hundred meters below.

He saw a long, rugged, brown-green landmass all alone in the endless immensity of Fillippi's ocean. The island was six hundred kilometers in length, eight to a hundred kilometers wide. North and South Bosom were separated by a mountain range—triple-peaked

Crasnus. He wouldn't see South Bosom; Crasnus blocked the view. But he saw the City of Simalta nestling against its side. He saw the industrial district north of the city and the space port next to it; a transport saucer lay there loading levitron for movement to the deep-space freighter anchored in orbit beyond the sunlight.

As his eyes passed over the panorama, he saw a tiny glinting off the island's far shore. He could see across Faltara at this point because Dominus was anchored at the narrowest point of the island, the so-called "Neck" where South and North Bosom met. At first he thought it was a large mother-bol come to the surface for an insect, but the glinting was repetitious, rhythmic. It seemed to have an intentional quality. Then it stopped. Drusilla studied the water, but he saw nothing more. He decided it must have been a quirk, perhaps a floating bottle bobbled by the waves in a rhythmic fashion. He turned his thoughts back to the challenge and stalked off toward his offices.

2 — AN IRRESISTIBLE OFFER

Ronald Frederick, the notorious Empire master spy, was seen entering the Ministry of the Interior under heavy guard today. Frederick was sentenced last year to life imprisonment in Hundro Fortress. Agency spokesmen insist that Frederick's visit was for routine interrogation.

—The Pappacappolus Capitol Observer

The rhythmic glinting Drusilla had observed was a signal from a submarine to a fishing boat. The fishing boat had waited for the signal since the early morning hours, and when its owner saw the sunlight reflected in a mirror, he roused his helpers and hoisted the red sail.

On the submarine, a man dressed in a grey jump-suit stood on the deck next to an open hatch. Hand raised to shade his eyes, he looked at the shoreline, cliffs rising steeply from the water, and a papla forest that came all the way to the drop-off. High above the conical papla crowns, Dominus hung in the sky. It was very far away, but the man recognized the familiar silhouette of the levitating city and saw as a grey blurr the slanting plane formed by hundreds of cables that held Dominus anchored to the flinty under-sea shelf of Faltara.

The Siege of Faltara was clearly underway.

The man now turned his attention to the approaching boat. It ran before a light breeze, its red sail almost slack, its aged hull a dull silver. Old Quantus stood in the bow, waving a fisherman's beret.

The man on the submarine was middle-sized, muscular, and gave the impression of taut intensity and collected strength. He had a weathered, leathery face—the islanders called it a "sea face"—and blue eyes that suggested inner calm, a kindly disposition, and a sense of humor. Black hair, needled in white and worn short, covered his rounded, massive head. He was just this side of forty.

On this planet he was known as Penta Mart, and all believed him a native of Fillippi. In fact his name was Ronald Frederick; he had been born on a world loyal to Empire and had served Empire's intelligence establishment until another fate had overtaken him six years ago. Now he was the leader of Cush—well known by name and reputation but not easily recognized by most of the people he served. He made sure of that.

Now his eyes grew merry and sparkled with a greenish flash. The boat came alongside, and Mart greeted Quantus, a toothless, silver-haired old man. Then he picked up a canvas bag filled with Phila for the Women's Crusade, called down the hatch to say that he was off, and jumped on board the fishing boat.

Quantus had ferried Mart to the island many a year now—ever since Cush had finished its submarine, a vessel made from stolen metal. He demonstrated his friendship with the famous man with kisses and embraces. His two young crewmen had never met Mart before and were clearly overawed. They shuffled their feet, wiped hands on collarless, armless red smocks, and pulled long braids in some embarrassment. Soon they withdrew to the back of the boat to get it underway again, while Quantus and his guest sat down on piles of folded sacks and began a time-honored conversation.

"You're getting younger, Quantus. You look very well, very well, old lox. How does the shaman run these days? How is bol fishing? You all set for the siege?"

"If you men of Cush would do your job, there wouldn't be a siege to get set for, that's what I say. When is the big day?"

"Don't hurry it, Quantus. When the revolution is victorious, you'll be sorry. You'll have to work twice as hard, and you won't have any excuses any longer. Nowadays when the shaman doesn't run, it's Concession's fault, right?"

Thus they chatted while the boat tacked to left and right and the shore approached. As they came nearer, Mart carried his bag to the bow of the boat. In a moment his eyes found the narrow path cut into the cliff leading up to the paplas above. Below the path an ancient dock stood on blackened, rotting stumps.

The bitter-sweet odor of *lacrema veni* came with the breeze; Mart breathed its odor with pleasure. It was Faltara's scent, his first impression of the planet.

When they were within meters of the dock, he said farewell to Quantus and waved to Quantus' men. He leaped off the boat before it touched the dock. Then, canvas bag under his arm, he began to climb the rockface. Halfway up he turned again and waved to the red sail below.

Hidden in the papla forest waited a yellow floater, its levitron tanks full, its jet in order, its trunk filled with Mart's various disguises. He could turn into any sort of man in a hurry—a lac farmer, a tundratus, a fompus, a laborer. He drove the floater through the forest until he emerged on Highway 1, Faltara's main north-south artery. He turned the floater right—south—with a hiss of side valves. Then the floater picked up speed as it moved over the dusty road.

Forest pressed in on either side. Sometimes the ocean gleamed green to Mart's right through the trees. Sometimes he glimpsed the levitating city high and distant to his left. Simalta lay ahead. He estimated his arrival—accounting for the stop-off on the way—in the early afternoon.

Faltara brought memories . . . of the beginning. The years with the people of Fillippi had made the planet his home, and of the seven large islands—not counting Gash, the military stronghold—he loved Faltara most. Not only had he landed here, but Faltara was a beauty: her rugged, rocky, wild North Bosom; her gentle, rolling, South Bosom; dark, massive Crasnus in the middle between them; and Simalta in the lap of Crasnus, a jewel of a city—all this shone with color and with life.

He would be sad when—soon—the time would come to leave. He could imagine how the planet would look from outer space—a radiant blue-white ball bathed in the light of old man Mo. Only a fool would leave this place to take up the old profession—after the inevitable court-martial he faced upon his return. Even if he succeeded in stealing the saucer, the commissars back home would find the shape of his last six years "irregular," to say the least. A court-martial was a certainty.

And yet . . . And yet, he would return. He was a party man and an Empire agent, and a man didn't change his stripes in the middle of his life.

*   *   *

Six years ago he had been on Pappacappolus, headquarters planet of Commercial System out here in the

Rim, pretending to be the president of a small out-space component testing service. He had come to Pappa with a mission—to steal the plans for System's Scout Saucer V—specifically the plans for its ion-shielding armature. Years of work had preceded his arrival; a very fine cover operation had been established. Mart soon made progress. He established contacts with the Navy's R&D command, and his flawless command of the latino tongue, his obvious technical expertise, and his native charm soon earned him appropriate contracts and increasingly better access to the Navy's computer system. At times he felt that his progress was too easy and too swift—and as it turned out later, it was. He had walked into a trap.

He was arrested six months after his arrival and endured a spectacular trial. Then he was taken to Hundro Fortress to last out the rest of his life. Hundro was a monstrosity of stone built in the feudal style that swept all civilizations at intervals of a thousand years. He lived in a dark hall with clay underfoot and giant, sweating stones as walls. All those about him were either madmen or political prisoners or both; some had languished in those caverns so long that they had forgotten both their names and their crimes. Mart's morale held for a while—but not for the entire year of his imprisonment. Toward the end he had resolved to kill himself by starvation rather than to endure the years in darkness. He sat in a corner, growing thin; only his eyes shone, deep in their sockets. And then came deliverance.

Two guards entered the stinking darkness one day. They shone light into the demented faces of those forgotten creatures down below until they found Mart. They took him out, told him to shave, to dress. A barber removed most of his hair. Then he was placed into a levi-limo and whisked three hundred kilometers to the heart of one of Pappa's administrative centers. The minister of the Interior wished to speak to him, he was told. He was told nothing else.

The Interior Ministry on Pappa was a sixteen-building complex with a multi-story needle in the center. High up in the needle ruled Hondo Thackus, the minister himself, a big, hairy outdoors man and famous hand-ball player. He waited for Mart behind an enormous desk. He wore a white, knee-length robe.

Mart entered the big man's presence and stood for a moment or two while Thackus flipped rapidly through a report. They were in an oval office filled with bar-bells, punching bags, a treadmill, and other machinery of exercise. Couches, chairs, and tables were conspicuous by absence. Trophies won by Thackus crowded wall shelves.

Mart looked uneasily at all of these symbols of excess energy. He himself was haggard and felt weak. His eyes had crawled back into their sockets, his cheeks were caves, and he had frightened himself in the mirror that morning when removing his lice-infested thatch. Through a tinted window behind the minister, he saw a part of Pappa cascading down the Five Hills toward the sea—an artfully random arrangement of chalkstone buildings interspersed by clumps of palms.

With an abrupt motion, Thackus pushed the report aside. He came around the desk with the vehemence of a rhino, jumped up on a treadmill, and started its machinery. As the belt began to move, he began to run. Only then did he look at Mart.

"Ever hear of the planet Fillippi?" Thick, brown, hairy legs were churning. Thackus did not wait for a reply. "Of course you have," he said. "You chaps in

Empire love nothing better than squeezing propaganda-juice from that mess. God, how you squeeze! Right? Right. Your policy is very contradictory. You love that planet for its propaganda value—and yet you fight like fools to take it from us. And if it weren't a flower planet, I'd let you have the place, my friend. It's a bloody nuisance. But we need the levitron as much as you do. I'm told that the price of lac is thirty thousand credits a liter these days. Up, up, up,'' he said, evidently referring to the price.

He reached forward and increased the speed of the belt while Mart still struggled to understand. He knew about Fillippi, the slave planet—a good example of what could happen when you sold planets as if they were apples.

"Levitron," Thackus cried. "Wonderful stuff. We need it *more* than you chaps. We have more heavy planets than you do, and fewer hydrocarbon planets. See what I mean?''

Mart saw what Thackus meant—it was obvious. Levitron could cut the energy requirements of a transportation system by thirty percent or more on certain planets. But he wished that the minister would come to the point.

"Fillippi is more than you think, Commissar. It's not only a flower planet, not only a nest of slave-holders as your propaganda keeps reminding us, it's also the only planet with a levitating city. And they have Menoma, a really curious little stuff.''

"A levitating city? In the *air?*'' Mart was astounded. This he hadn't heard.

"In the *air?*'' Thackus mocked. "Of course, in the air. Where else would a city levitate to if you poured it full of levitron? Yes, Commissar, in the air. Dominus. That's the name of the place. Dominus dominates. The boys on Fillippi are anything but subtle—or I should say the degenerate Contortus family. They run the place. It used to be a floating city. Fillippi is a water planet. They filled the air tanks with levitron, and up, up, up she goes. Eight or nine hundred meters into the air. The trade winds drive it around the planet. Very convenient. It goes from island to island to suck up levitron. It takes a million liters of lac juice to keep Dominus up there, and the stuff has to be renewed once a year. Guess what percentage of Fillippi's production that is?"

"Sizeable, I'd say."

"Indeed, it is. Twenty-five percent of production. The lac industry around here is going to pieces over such waste. After all there are only sixteen such planets in Outermost, and six of them belong to you chaps. But you know the rules we go by in System. Don't interfere with the concessions. It's the very basis of our constitution."

"I understand that you *can* interfere," Mart said.

"Sure we can, Commissar. But only if they stop paying taxes. Or if they refuse to deliver troop levies on command. The Fillippi Concession is very good about those things. They pay the taxes—and they can afford to. And their troops arrive on Riondi in good order. They're full of Menoma, of course, but our military people don't seem to mind that."

Mart also knew about Riondi. It was a bleak, nearly waterless planet in the same solar system as Fillippi. By mutual agreement, System and Empire fought for Fillippi on Riondi. Nothing to destroy there. But Menoma? That was something new.

"Menoma?" he asked. "What is it? A drug?"

"Curious little stuff, Menoma. Interferes with the memory. You take it and you don't remember. For instance, you don't remember you're Commissar Frederick, a man condemned to die. You don't remember a thing. You don't remember how to walk, either, but there are ways to fix that. Works a little like a drug-gun—and *you* know how those work. That's a favorite weapon of spooks like you. But Menoma has more clout.''

Mart understood vaguely. Menoma must be used to undergird the slave culture. This was news again. He said:

''You're telling me that a member of the System Federation is violating the Galactic Drug Accords—and that you're not doing anything about it. Don't you think that that's a little risky?''

Thackus smiled. His tanned face was beginning to bead up from his exertions. He reached forward and pushed up the speed of his belt another notch.

''Not at all, Commissar. Let me remind you once again. You're a condemned man. Who're you going to tell? Surely you don't think you're headed home, do you? And by the time you get done with the Fillippi Concession, that little violation of the GDA will be a thing of the past.''

''When *I* get done with the . . .''

''Of course—you. Who else? Why do you think I'm telling you all this? I'm not a travel agency.''

''What precisely have you got in mind?''

''We want you to go in there and topple the Concession. Very simple, really. A refusal to pay taxes, a denial of troops for the war on Riondi . . . Better yet, a call for System to come in. But if you call System, the call must come from the leader of the Concession.''

''But how in the world do you think I can do that?''

''Why, by revolution. How else? It seems to me that

you're a little dense, Commissar—for a man with your credentials.''

"You mean—build a revolutionary apparatus, take over the Concession, that sort of thing? That could take years.''

"You have plenty of time, Commissar. Your alternative is jail—forever. And we have plenty of time too. This administration has another six years to go. We want to impact on the next general election.''

The minister clicked off the treadmill and hopped off. He danced over to a punching bag, moving like a boxer, and began to belabor the device with powerful, driving blows.

"But why me? Why not one of your own people?''

Pow, pow, pow went the minister's fists. He paused. "You're a citizen of Empire and not subject to our constitution. That's why. How do you think this administration would fare if we took steps to remove one of the concessions by force or fraud?'' Pow, pow, pow, he went against the bag. "That's how,'' he said. "Finished. Knockout. Fillippi has already cost us the entire liberal wing.'' Pow. "Our expansion among the uncommitted planets of Outermost has come to a standstill—thanks to your propaganda.'' Pow, pow, pow. "The Fillippi Concession must go—but it must go legally. We will uphold the constitution and also maintain our conservative support, the only support we have left. Got it?'' He went into a frenzy of punches.

Mart waited until Thackus was done. Then he said, "I don't understand you entirely. If the lac industry is behind you, why can't you just move in—regardless of the constitution. Go in over the violation of the drug accords.''

Thackus had transferred himself to some bar-bells.

He had bent down to pick up a pair from the red carpet, and now he looked up from a bent-over position. "You Empire chaps are really quite childish about politics." he said and rose. He began to pump the bar-bells forward and back, his arm muscles flexing.

"We can't just dash in there and take out the Fillippi Concession like a rotting oyster from its shell. That's how you do it on your side, but we don't have that luxury. We can't dictate what time-collapse will beam. The lac industry—why, that's only three percent of the Gross Region Product. Our conservatives won't stand still for interference with a concession, not even the Fillippi Concession."

He paused with his pumping for a second and lowered his arms.

"I'm under severe pressures to remove that blight and get more lac into the pipeline—but I'm supposed to do it by prayer. Prayer, Commissar."

"So you support some kind of operation I might start," Mart said. "What difference does that make? That's hair splitting."

"You've got it all wrong, Commissar. We don't support you. We don't back you in any way. You'll be a free entrepreneur. That's what you pretended to be when you slipped onto this planet, right? Well, you can do some more of that. We won't even know that you are there. How can we help it if Empire sends an agitator to Fillippi? That's lamentable, but not our fault. Understand me?"

"How do you know that I won't just take off and go home?"

"You might try to walk," Thackus said, "but short of that you might have trouble. The merchant captains who make the Fillippi run will know all about you, and so will the military chaps on Riondi. You won't even get *near* a space ship."

Thackus moved to a bicycle and began to pedal furiously. The speedometer on the rig showed forty kilometers an hour.

"What do *I* get out of this?"

"Well, sir," Thackus answered, his breath coming hard from the exertion, "if you deliver Fillippi before our term is up, we give you a ticket to the nearest Empire planet."

"How do I know that you will keep your side of the bargain?"

"How do I know that you can do the job? And, besides that, Commissar, you're a condemned man, right? Right. Better to be on Fillippi in the sun than in Hundro Fortress. It's a terrible hotel and a worse home. If I'm still here when you report back, I personally guarantee your return."

Thackus stretched out his right hand while his left remained on the handle bar and his legs went around and around.

Mart hesitated.

"Come on, man," Thackus said, and he moved his outstretched hand in the air. "I'm making you an offer you can't refuse. Shake. Come on and shake."

3 — PHILA AND OTHER MATTERS

*We must find an antidote. While they have Menoma
and we have nothing, we're dead. If there is a drug,
there is an antidote. There must be a man on this planet
who understands lac chemistry. Let's go out and find
him.*

> —Penta Mart at his first staff
> meeting on Fillippi

Penta Mart pulled the floater off the road, stopped,
and got out. Three youngsters drove a herd of ryant
cattle toward the north, whips cracking. The animals
crowded the narrow road—a mass of yellow bodies
covered with long, dusty hair, the sturdy heads with
triple horns just off the ground. Mart smiled as the boys
passed. They would hide the cattle from raiding tundrati in the rocky heights of North Bosom. The Siege
was on.

Up ahead a transport saucer rose into the sky resplendent in an envelope of energy. Suddenly it picked
up speed and changed direction; then came the sonic
boom.

Mart resumed his ride, his thoughts on Hondo
Thackus. Thackus now campaigned to be Prime Minister, and Mart followed the campaign by way of a
time-collapse receiver installed at Cush's Polar Camp.
The press hounded Thackus at every occasion about

Fillippi. Fillippi had been Thackus' weak point six years ago, it was his failure now. If Mart succeeded in his venture, as he guessed he would, the fall of Fillippi Concession would ensure Thackus' election—which Empire would thoroughly appreciate. They'll boil me in oil, Mart thought.

The dust raised by the cattle settled and the visibility improved. Soon he would pass the port where he had landed five years ago, arriving as a stow-away in a specially constructed crate. During his first night on the planet, he had cut his way to freedom using a small beam saw. A time-delay thermal bomb had destroyed his crate and much of the warehouse, and that fire had signalled the birth of Cush. His situation had been hopeless, but he had been determined to succeed against all odds—and by then he knew exactly what he faced.

Back on Pappa, bureaucrats had briefed him about the planet in a series of gruelling sessions. He recalled a meeting where they flashed eight hundred and sixty-nine slides on the screen. The number still stuck in his mind. He had learned what he could about the people, the economy, the politics of Castle, key personalities, history, geology, flora, fauna.

Fillippi came across conventional enough. Empire would have called it "pre-bourgeois"—a backward planet with a small population and limited resources (the sea teemed with minerals, but it took energy to get them out of it). The government was feudal and repressive—a common feature of System worlds; System had many "company planets." The people were sturdy, healthy, hardy and devoted themselves entirely to fishing, lac raising, and cattle. Fillippi lacked universities, industry, and communications media. The people were too poor to plug into the time-collapse. An off-planet corporation ran the lac refinery under a long-term contract.

During his briefings, Mart asked repeatedly about Menoma. His questions led to a special session on the drug. A balding ministry scientist who peered uncertainly over bifocals gave the briefing. He explained the chemical with the help of graphics projected on a screen.

Menoma, said the scientist, was a complex organic molecule—more complex than levitron itself and even more resistant to synthetic production. Trillions of credits had been spent attempting to produce levitron in a lab—without success. No one had even tried to make Menoma or an antidote.

Mart listened patiently for a while, but as the lecture bogged down in technical detail, he cut in.

"In essence then—Menoma destroys memory?"

"Erases memory," the chemist said.

"Erases memory," Mart conceded. "You say there is no antidote?"

"Unfortunately not."

Mart stared at a chart of the awesome Menoma molecule recalling films of Menoma slaves—their eyes glazed, their features dehumanized, their talk mechanical.

"Tell me," he said, addressing the scientist, "how can the Concession program people so effectively after they take Menoma?"

"Well, sir," the chemist said, "the subjects become like babies again. Their minds turn receptive. They absorb all information without question—as in hypnosis. They turn into sponges, as it were."

"Do they become *really* effective?"

"That's a function of the information they receive. A few weeks on conditioning tapes and in kinesthetic machines can't duplicate years of sensory experience. As a rule Menoma subjects are inefficient and disfunctional, but in a specific area—especially if it's a simple skill—they can become quite proficient.''

"What they lose in efficiency, they make up for in absolute obedience. They function well enough on Riondi.'' The speaker was a military expert in the group, and his tone was admiring.

"And, of course, with the passage of time, they learn new skills in the ordinary way,'' the chemist said. "We suspect that the brain retains some kind of very deep memory. They learn to walk, talk, and move remarkably quickly, better than you would expect. And there is Menoma madness—two in ten are subject to it. The subject appears to remember something and usually goes beserk. So there is evidence of some obscure remembrance, hence we say that the memory is erased rather than destroyed.''

Mart had arrived on Fillippi knowing that he must find an antidote to Menoma. The drug was fed to every person drawn into Concession service—thousands of people every year, most of them young men inducted into the tundrati. Fompa, officers, and managers of enterprises were recruited in other ways. Menoma had a serious limitation: its victims lost initiative and the ability to make complex decisions. Concession's higher-ranking servants were men and women who worked for money, power, and privilege. They were fully human and therefore subject to persuasion. Not so Menoma slaves.

A year after his arrival, Mart found a man willing to tackle the problem. He was Para Ligg, a young mathematician and member of the repressed Tesso cult. He claimed that mathematics could solve any problem—and Mart gave him Menoma by way of a challenge. Ligg worked for three years on the geometry of the Menoma molecule, seeking ways to destroy its symmetry. In that time Mart built up the hard core of a revolutionary organization.

Then came a day Mart was not likely to forget. Ligg had sent a message that he might have found the anti-dote. Like Menoma itself, it was a fractional distillate of *lacrema veni.* Instead of using mathematics, Ligg had stumbled on the formula.

Ligg and his young wife lived in two rooms in an old house off Trippani square, the oldest part of Simalta. Mart and a number of his senior leaders stood in the kitchen by a window with a view of Crasnus. A clump of Nary pines nearby sent a rich aroma into the air. The center of attention was a furry tree-baguse madly swinging in a home-made wooden cage. Ligg fed it a greenish pap. Then he injected Menoma into the beast's arm.

Shocked by the drug, the tree-baguse fell to the floor and lay on sawdust amidst half-chewed kirrus rinds. If the antidote failed, the animal would behave like a newborn upon awakening, capable only of sucking motion.

An hour passed. From time to time the young Tessori told them that all was right. Then the small monkey stirred, moved, jumped up, whistled, chirped, and held out a claw for food. Ligg gave it a stone button. The tree baguse spat angrily and took up a shrill cry.

The people stood in silence. Then they too came to life—embracing, yelling, crying. The celebration lasted until morning and consumed ten bottles of green cicillo wine. Only Ligg didn't drink. He was a man of the Way. He didn't touch alcohol and sipped lac tea.

They named the drug "Phila" that night. It was the

name of Para Ligg's young wife. In the Latin tongue it stood for kindness.

Mart slowed down his floater. In a still-hidden clearing to his left, he hoped to see the Fangano family's silver-and-green levitron chopper—and Balto Fangano himself.

The chopper was there. Next to it two men in green jump-suits rummaged in a tool box. Seated on a tree trunk some distance ahead of the aircraft loomed the large, bearlike figure of Lord Balto Fangano. He rose when he saw Mart's floater. He wore rumpled, grey overalls and thick-soled mountain boots.

Mart smiled and waved. He called Balto "my gift from Felicitas," a statement that amused his staff. His staff said that Penta worked his heart out for an objective, but when he achieved it, he gave all the credit to the "Great Serendipity."

"Penta Mart," Balto cried. Then he bent down to anchor Mart's floater to a root. "You've made it," he said, rising again. "How was the trip? How is it under the ice?" The voice was deep and resonant. It issued from a barrel of a chest and had that kind of sound.

Mart jumped from the floater and the men shook hands.

"It's cold in Polar Camp, as usual," Mart said. "And the trip was long and boring, as usual. But it's nice to see you, big man. I am glad that you could meet me. Has the challenge been delivered?"

Balto nodded. The two men sat down on nearby stumps, their backs toward the oblong, silvery Fangano chopper. Balto's two men stood on its roof now, oiling jet pivots. In front of Mart the yellow floater described a lazy circle in the air around its anchor.

"We sent the challenge five days ago," Balto rumbled. Then he chuckled. "Soon after that all hell broke loose. Armies of fake maintenance men tried to fix all sorts of leaks. Drusilla's goons tried to bribe our servants, and others tried to negotiate—but we threw them out, of course. Leo has things under control. But what about your end? Is everything on schedule? Have you found a good tafchuko yet?"

Mart frowned and shook his head. "That little chore is still ahead—and I'll need a lot of luck. Only a fool of a tafchuko would join our cause—the way Concession pampers that lot."

"They swim in privilege," Balto said. "But they are patriots, or so I'm told. Tafchuko manhood, that sort of thing. That tradition is older than the Concession."

Great traditions had a way of fading, Mart thought, and men whose spirit had conquered the planet had great-great-grandsons who sang another tune.

"When I first came to Fillippi," he said, "I thought that they would be my natural allies. I was wrong. Not a single tafchuko has joined Cush—and God knows I've tried. The Castle has bought them out. It's like the lac workers. If you are under Concession's protection and if your children are exempt from the Tower, you don't rock the boat."

"How will you do it—the recruiting?"

Mart shrugged. "I don't know. I'll just have to trust It." He pointed to the sky, meaning the Great Serendipity.

Balto smiled. "Knowing you, 'It' will drop a tafchuko right into your lap. I dropped into your lap, remember?"

Now it was Mart's turn to smile. "It took me three days of argument to bring you around, my friend. I landed you, Balto, but it was more like catching a mother-bol with a six-kilo line.

For a moment they were silent. Then Balto spoke. "Look here, Penta. We don't need a good tafchuko to train me. I've been riding tafpa every morning—including this morning. Can't you smell it? I reek like a genuine tafchuko. And I'm getting pretty good at it, too. And Ignazio doesn't impress me."

Mart looked dubious. "Ignazio is just a puppet, but Drusilla is a snake. And he *does* impress me. Blubber-boy has never lost a duel. He has fought thirty-three without an injury. Thirty-three. If I didn't know that Drusilla is lurking in the background, I would think that uncanny. But Drusilla is there. 'Seven Lives' had a lot of help in all those duels; otherwise he would be two meters under by now."

"He has never fought a tafpa joust."

"True," Mart said, "but I wouldn't count on that too much. My guess is that they will have some trouble rigging a tafpa joust—and that's why I insisted on that form of combat. But they will try to rig it nonetheless. If they use some kind of drug to put steel up that sissy's spine, he might survive five rounds. And if he does, we are back where we started. I wanted a form of combat they had never used before—but it has that drawback. It's a traditional sport with traditional rules. And that's why we must try to get you the best damn trainer we can find. And buy a first-rate animal. Those nags in your stables . . ." He shook his head with disapproval.

"That's all set," Balto said. "Leo has made reservations for the Potsla Run auction."

"Good." Then Mart wiped his forehead. "God," he said. "How time flies. That's just a month away. I have to find my tafchuko soon. By the time he comes to you, I want him trained as a Cush operative. And I want him at the auction. I don't trust your eye for tafpas.

Which reminds me. Any applicants for tafpa-master in your household?''

Balto grinned. ''No. At the salary we advertised, all the masters up in Castle should be drooling at our gate. Drusilla must have gotten out the word.''

''Until his candidate arrives.''

Balto chuckled.

''Well,'' Mart said, ''that seems to be working.''

Balto shook his head wonderingly and smiled. ''Nefarious, nefarious. What an idea. To *let* them infiltrate a spy . . .''

''An old tactic.'' Mart said. ''I just hope that Drusilla doesn't catch on. If he falls for it—even temporarily—he will waste a lot of his time trying to make his man effective—instead of seeking many channels of intelligence.''

''He is doing that now.''

''Yes. But he doesn't have an agent in the house at present. Did you tell Leo how to deal with the man?''

''I always follow my orders to the letter, Penta, like a good revolutionary.''

''I'm in something of a hurry,'' Mart said, ''so let's talk about a change in tactics. You remember the old plan?'' Balto nodded. ''Well, I want to make a change. It's designed to put more pressure on Drusilla, to keep him off balance. When all the families go down to the Fair Grounds, you and your people will stay away. Until the day before the joust. Make sure that space is reserved for you, but don't put up the tents. That'll give Drusilla something to worry about for three weeks or so.''

''Where will we stay? On Dominus?''

''No. You'll disappear. One of our supporters has a secluded ranch in South Bosom big enough to accommodate most of your household. You'll be training there in secret. Drusilla isn't likely to find you, not right away, and he'll be wondering where you are.''

Mart rose from his stump. He reached into one of the zippered pockets of his jump-suit and brought out three sheets of folded paper. ''Give these to Leo and have him start the planning. This has all the details. I suggest that he move the family during the Potsla Run auction. If my guess is right, everybody will be there to see the action, and Drusilla will be preoccupied. You'll be there too, of course. No one will be watching your household.''

Balto took the papers, glanced at them, nodded. ''When do we meet next?''

''Probably on the ranch, after the auction.'' Mart said, ''I'll send you a message through the tafchuko— should I be so lucky to find one. Or I might communicate with you through Fompus Richter. The tafchuko, by the way, will come to you disguised as a tundratus—a replacement for one of your palace guards. He will insist on seeing you personally. The recognition phrase will be 'east gate'.''

Balto smiled. ''Nefarious,'' he said. ''Sooo nefarious. 'East Gate' it is.''

''Well, I'm off, Balto old friend. I've got a sackful of Phila to deliver—thirteen herb shops. Then I'll have a session with Richter. His part of the show starts in a month, as you know, and there are still hundreds of loose ends. That's the risky part of the operation. If things go wrong in Richter's operation—and on the other islands—we have virtually no contingency plan. After I'm done with Richter, there is still a tafchuko to be found, and I still haven't given up on the Contortus palace. We have to get an agent in there *and* out of there.''

''I thought you had an agent there.''

"I did," Mart said. "Veronica Dox. She's dead. One of our people saw her in the waste pipes. Dead and tortured. I can't keep them alive in there."

Balto looked grim. "Death to the menace," he rumbled.

"Death to the menace," Mart said and nodded. Then they shook hands and parted.

Mart drove off again, thinking of Balto, his gift from Felicitas.

Finding the Fangano family had been a stroke of luck—earned by hard work, like all luck. Mart's staff had watched the Castle lords for years before the Fangano name had suddenly surfaced—a new and minor family rumored not to use Menoma slaves and with a lord in charge who liked to spend his days down on the islands among the little people and amidst great rocks. A curious family, a family to keep your eye on.

Mart had watched the family for some months before he dared approach Balto Fangano on one of the small "rocks" that formed the Illoppo chain. Cush had some pseudo-camps in the Illoppos maintained by a handful of volunteers to focus Concession's military interest. The real Cush camp lay beneath the northern pole.

Mart learned that the Fanganos wished to leave Fillippi if only they could. "We were taken," Balto told him. "We didn't know the truth about Fillippi. We didn't know that it was a vipers' nest. All we saw was a bargain—thirty million credits for a share in a flower planet! Unheard-of in New Frontier. We jumped at it. Now we know better—but we can't find a soul who wants to buy us out."

The Fanganos were quiet, respectable merchants—not heroes. When Mart proposed that Balto lead a revolution against the iron grip of the Contortus family,

the Lord Fangano declined politely—although with
evident hesitation and with expressions of regret. And
when Mart saw that hesitation, that regret, he knew he
had a chance. He went to work on Balto in earnest. His
plans demanded an ally among the concessionaires,
and Balto was his best bet. When at last Balto put his
bearlike paw in Mart's hand, Mart had known Cush
could win. Now, more than ever, he was certain of it.

The forest ended abruptly, and Mart saw spread out
before him the colorful panorama of Simalta—pastel-
shade buildings against the dark, triple-peaked
backdrop of Crasnus. The city's core—or new city—
stood in the valley: a cluster of highrise buildings,
including Concession's headquarters on the island, the
Tower. Farther south, rising up into the foothills of the
mountain, stood an old city. Most of the herb shops
were located there; most of the people lived there.

As he drove on through the northern industrial district, past silvery lac refineries to his right and giant
golden levitron storage globes on his left, he reflected
that it would be a long day.

4 — A SUMMONED TESSORI

Let every choice be truly your choice. There is no error when you are deliberate. The world will uphold you if you act from the Center. You cannot die.
    —*Tesso of Hallisma, Fundamentals 8:21*

As Mart arrived at Mother Nola's herb shop, sunset had begun to shroud Trippani square in darkness. He stepped from the floater and hooked its chain into a parking ring set in one of the thick cartana trees that stood like guards around the square and hid from view ancient buildings of carved stone.

From the Sea Dragon down the street came the drunken roar of the tundrati. Five hundred men had waded across the beach from hydrofoils today— enough to give the Castle lords a sense of security. The mindless howling came from some of those.

In the square people played dead: not a glint of light behind those concave windowpanes. Only one lamp splashed orange waves across the rounded cobblestones and touched the dry fountain in the middle of the square: Mother Nola's lantern. Nola was a fearless old crone. Mart had heard a story about her to the effect that several tundrati had tried to wreck her shop once; but her trenchant gaze had penetrated their Menoma stupidity and they had slunk out of her place like chastened dogs.

Mart reached for his canvas bag. He felt weary and yet the night had just begun. He had to visit three more shops tonight, change his disguise, and then see Fompus Richter. The search for that elusive tafchuko would have to wait another day.

He walked toward the orange light thinking that a man's luck had a good deal to do with his levels of energy. He didn't feel very lucky tonight.

A pair of eyes watched Mart as he disappeared into the shop, a young girl's eyes. Her name was Sophie Han. She stood half hidden by a tree. She had waited in the shadow of that cartana for nearly an hour now, undecided. In a way she welcomed the man's arrival. It gave her more time to think. She still hesitated. Her feelings still boiled and bubbled vehemently. She was not behaving like a true tessori and sought cool calm in order to reach the right decision.

She was tastefully but plainly dressed—so much so that her shapely charms were somewhat muted. She was setting out on a very long journey but carried nothing but a purse. A month ago she had reported to the Concession Tower in the new part of Simalta. Menoma slaves had herded her with other young women into a dark and grimy hall with low benches against the wall. The air reeked with the invisible ethers of fear. A voice crackling through a faulty intercom system told them to undress and form a line before a door—by now a routine procedure for Sophie Han. She had done the same thing every year since age eleven; it was part of the registration process, part of the procedure whereby Castle chose its slaves.

She had walked through the door into the glare of

spotlights on a stage. Two slaves operated a film camera on wheels, while a young fompus in flowing robes eyed the naked young women, evidently pleased by their discomfort. He began to stroll up and down before them and stopped in front of Sophie. He looked at her for a moment with a leer. "Castle-bait," he said, more to himself than to her. "Get lots of film on this one," he told the filming slaves. "Get up close to her and get some angles."

Ever since that time, Sophie Han had known that she'd be summoned. She had prepared herself for that eventuality. She had been certain that she would meet the situation with equanimity. When the Summons had arrived five days ago ordering her to report to the Tower today, no later than midnight, she had accepted that fate without a stir of emotion. She had decided that she would go to Mother Nola for a dose of Phila and get it over with—but now that she stood here, she had second thoughts.

Hers was not much of a choice. She could report to the Tower, would be fed Menoma, and would turn into a mindless but obliging lump, her spirit imprisoned in a body but no longer hers.

Or alternatively, she could swallow Phila—but she didn't want to die. Not yet. Her spirit would be free to roam—but she loved *this* life and knew little about the next.

On the one hand—the Teachings forbade suicide. On the other hand—the Master had written: "You are Spirit and ultimately all choice is yours. Dogma serves your spirit, not spirit dogma." She could remain loyal to the Teachings even in their breach . . .

Her thoughts returned compulsively to that scene in the Tower—the shivering girls under those bright, harsh beams, their bodies light and shadow; the prancing fompus and his leering face; the dull Menoma slaves at work on the camera; the reek of fear and desperation in the air.

Why had she been chosen this time and not before? She was pretty at age twenty, but no prettier than at seventeen, eighteen, nineteen.

She could only think of one explanation. This time she was in love. Love had made her body radiate up on that stage despite all attempts to look as sexless as a . . . as a cobblestone.

Thoughts of Jan now overwhelmed her—a sweet-sad panic of loss and longing. Tears caught and squeezed her throat. She had a sudden urge to run away from here, to rush off into darkness—somewhere, anywhere, just away from here.

But no. She couldn't do it. Failure to report would mean the forcible enslavement of her family and probably of her friends as well. She couldn't yield to panic; she had to concentrate and make a choice. Jan—he was behind her. Jan, poor Jan. She hadn't had the heart to tell him. Others would do that—gently. Gently—and only after her departure. He might be more resigned and less likely to harm himself or others in that case.

Sophie Han breathed in and out slowly and rhythmically. Gradually her emotions settled. Total darkness now enveloped Trippani square. She saw the man leaving the shop and watched him float away down a narrow alley. She continued breathing, in and out, in and out . . .

Then, quite without bidding, she felt an inner certainty. The Way had come into her calm and had shown her the way. She had decided. She set out across the square.

The shop lay below street level and she had to step down to get in. A bull-bell attached to the door startled her for a second, but she fell back into concentration. She looked about and ordered the shop in her mind: shelves all around were filled with hundreds of small bottles; a large counter faced the entrance; behind it a black curtain with astrological symbols in silver and in gold marked the door to a back room. Mother Nola stood before the curtain—a shrivelled form, an ancient head. A long needle penetrated the sparse, silvery bun of hair atop the ancient skull. Hard, dark eyes stared at Sophie Han.

Mother Nola took the young girl's measure. Blond, bosomy, and young. Around twenty. Nola's memory stirred. Sophie Han, she told herself, the young musician. She knew the Hans—members of the Tesso cult—mathematicians, musicians, and teachers of the Will. This girl before her—hesitating at the door, intimidated by the bell—had the tessori look about her: disciplined and inwardly collected.

I look like an old witch to her, Mother Nola thought. Her eyes rest on the golden ring in my left ear; she wonders how the earlobe got to be so long; she wonders how my hair could get so white; she thinks my hands resemble claws . . .

Nola felt a cool excitement, a spider's cool excitement. Could this female be the one? Penta Mart had just now urged her to find another agent for Drusilla's vicious keep. Veronica Dox was dead—her tortured body thrown out with the garbage of the lords. Cush needed this young tessori, this person schooled in moral culture, her mind cool as water from a well, her emotions leashed. Had the girl come seeking Phila? You could never tell with these cult people. Girls carrying the Summons usually had the tear-stained look. This girl was proud. She would make a very fine agent.

The girl came to the counter holding a purse before her as if it contained a precious object.

"Do you remember me?" she asked.

"I remember everyone I've ever seen," Mother Nola said. "You're Sophia Han. You're a musician. A year ago you came to me and wanted Phila. I refused you, as I recall. I suppose that you have the Summons now? I don't sell Phila to those who *might* be going to the Tower—only to those who're going."

"I've got it," Sophie said.

"Let me see it then, child. I must be sure."

The girl reached into her purse. It was made from seashells and clackered as she opened it. A nice white blouse, Nola noted, a red scarf around her neck, blue skirt with pleats. The simple, tessori look. She glanced at the girl's fingers. A musician, yes. The fingertips were calloused from the strings of the ballusa, the dulicet, the viola. Probably all three. Perfect, she thought. Richter's last message had said that the Contorti were seeking a musician for the entertainment troupe.

The girl handed a folded piece of paper over the counter, her blue eyes cool and self-assured.

Nola recognized the Summons even before she had unfolded the page. She looked up at the girl. "Why do you want Phila?"

"Must you know that?"

"Yes. Phila is not for everyone."

"I'd rather die than be a lump on Dominus."

"Do you think that Phila is a poison?"

"No," Sophie said. "But those who take both Phila and Menoma die. The drugs react with one another. They paralyze the heart."

"How do you know that?"

"Everyone says that."

And so they do, so they do, Mother Nola thought. Cush itself spread that rumor among the people. Cush only wanted people with high motivation. How could the movement send people to very likely death unless they had already decided to die?

"Does your family know that you are here?" Nola asked. "Do they know you plan to use Phila?"

"No. They'd disapprove."

"Why?"

"Because we—" The girl hesitated. "We don't believe in suicide."

"We?"

"My family, I mean."

"You're a tessori. You don't have to hide that from me. I approve, you know. I've lived in this neighborhood for eighty years; I know all about your cult. Don't worry, I won't turn you in. And I disapprove of suicide as much as the Master."

"Then why do you sell Phila?"

"Because it's not a poison."

The alert old eyes picked up the girl's surprise. Sophie's hand fluttered up and adjusted her blond locks. "What does it do, then?"

"It gives you awareness," Mother Nola said.

The girl hesitated and then spoke with scorn. "In the life after death?"

Nola was amused. "No. In your life here and now. Phila gives you your memory back."

Sophie's eyes moved like wind-stirred water, and Nola could almost hear the thoughts: *But . . . in that case . . . I'll live, I'll live, I'll be myself, this very me.* They all had the selfsame thought, experienced the selfsame shock. They came prepared for death and got life instead. Phila *was* kindness—but it called for courage.

"Is it an antidote?"

"Yes."

"But . . . but what good is that? Then I'll live through all the humiliation with, with my eyes open, as it were. I'd rather not remember than be a conscious harlot."

"Calm down," Nola said. "Phila is for those who're strong. And those who wish to serve. You need not become a harem girl; in fact, it's best if you don't. You'll lose your pretty hair, but that's a small price to pay."

"I don't understand you."

"Dominus has all kinds of slaves—they cook, they sew, they . . . play music. We'd rather that you be one of those, able to move about freely. Harem girls are under lock and key. They can't do much for us."

"Us?" Sophie asked.

"Haven't you guessed?"

"You mean . . . Cush? *You?* An Agent?"

Mother Nola nodded. "If you take Phila, you'll be one of us—and you'll have to work for us."

"Gladly," the girl said. Her eyes flashed.

"The work is dangerous," Nola warned. "You'll be risking your life."

"Gladly," Sophie repeated.

"You're certain?"

"I'm certain."

"Very well," Nola said. "We need an agent in the Contortus household, a musician. The girl you'll be replacing died of Menoma madness. If all goes well, you'll end up working for a certain Mistress Sultana—who is not one of us. We have no agents in that household. You'll be the only one—the eyes and ears of Cush. A man named Olaf, in the Tower, will tell you more about your assignment while you undergo conditioning. Listen to him carefully and do exactly what he says. He is tall. A cheerful man. Watch for him. Now let me have your Summons again.''

Nola made an obscure mark in a corner of the reddish sheet. "This will alert our friends in the Tower," she said, returning the paper. Then she fixed the young woman with a stare.

"Do you have a sweetheart?"

Sophie blushed. She has a boy, Nola decided. Even Tesso of Hallisma approved of love.

"You won't go to him," Nola said sternly. "You won't visit anyone. It's for your own good. Your life will be in constant danger up there in the castle. You may never return. It's best if all those dear to you believe that you're a Menoma slave."

Nola reached into her apron pocket and pulled out an oblong bluish capsule—Phila. She laid it on the counter.

"Wait here," she said. "I'll fetch you some tea to wash it down with."

5 — THE TAFCHUKO

The tafpa is an aberration of nature. It is a cross between a horse and a camel, but it has six legs, red eyes, and its fur is blue. To look at it you would think that it cannot walk—and it can't. It just hobbles about like a man on crutches. Yet it is the fastest land animal in Outermost. When aroused, its humps secrete a hormone, and the legs move so rapidly that they make a blurr.

—From *Popular Guide to Outermost Mutations*

About twelve or thirteen kilometers north-east of Trippani square, as the bird flies, Potsla Run sprawled over the country: Fillippi's most prestigious tafpa ranch.

Seen from the air, it made a rough, irregular T bordered by a papla forest. A road divided the stem of the T into two parts. Some distance from the chalkstone gates, on the left, a large columned mansion and its satellite buildings stood beneath a group of ancient trees. Three kilometers farther on, still on the left, guest houses made a circle, screened on all sides by Nary pines and flanked by gardens. From the houses the Auction Circle could be seen at the bottom of a gentle slope fringed by a dense wall of paplars.

The road went past the houses and rose to the top of a
hill, the Run's highest point, where a hunting lodge
dominated the scene. From it one could oversee the
rough terrain of the T's cross-bar, ideal country for the
lox chase and the felina hunt.

The right side of the ranch belonged to the tafpas.
They grazed over rolling fields marked off by white
fencing. At a level with the mansion, surrounded by
high wire fencing, stood stables for the most valuable
animals. And opposite the guest area, on a piece of
level ground, also outlined by a line of pines, was a
large oval field for racing and mock-jousts. Bleachers
overlooked the field on one side, and jousting dummies
marked either end of the field. Standing on the highest
bleacher one could see, some distance to the right, the
roof-tops of Potsla Village out of sight below a rise.
And beyond the racing oval, along the road, were more
corrals, more training ovals.

Despite its size and extent, the tafpa ranch gave off
an atmosphere of order and of wealth. The housekeep-
ing was meticulous, the facilities superb. White-
pebbled walks lead to various points on the Run. The
rich scent of flowers—mingling with tafpa odors—rose
from gardens scattered about the estate, each with its
fountain and trellised gazebo. The paint gleamed fresh
on buildings, barns, and stables. Vegetable fields in-
serted here and there between corrals were lush yet
geometrical. Tools and implements around the stables
and workshops were polished and new.

Now as dusk settled over the Run, people walked
toward Potsla Village from their various chores around
the estate. Several streams converged near the oval
jousting field and passed beyond it. The people talked
and laughed as if there were no Siege. Soon they were
out of sight, their voices a faint murmur. Lights came

on in the mansion and around the stables, and Dominus became a large brilliance, an immense star against the sky.

In the middle of the oval training field, all alone in the darkness, Jan Rigg finally decided to give up the struggle. It was too dark to see, despite the brilliance that came from Castle. He sat high in the saddle of a tafpa between the first and second humps of the beast. He wore a floppy canvas tafchuko hat, a ruffled white tafchuko shirt; he had on blue britches now stained with tafpa sweat, and on his legs he wore slender, tightfitting boots. In the darkness his features were obscured, but the silhouette of his face against the sky revealed a young man with a worried expression. He leaned forward now and patted the tafpa on the sweaty neck. Doing so, he shook his head sadly. Poor Glitsch, he thought. Poor Glitsch.

Glitsch was the finest tafpa Jan had trained in the last five years. The beast was incomparably fast. He responded to the merest pressure applied to flanks and humps. Glitsch could change pace—a violent sideways jump—like few other tafpas. He had energy, courage, and endurance. And it was all as it should be—no less had been predicted at his birth. He was descended from Potsla Run's finest line: his sire was Frotsch, his grand-sire Tluk, his great-grandsire the legendary Snart. On his forehead was the famous white marking shaped like an inverted V, the sign that had distinguished other fateful, famous animals.

Glitsch had everything a truly great jouster must have—except for one crucial detail. He shied from the lance.

Jan wished he knew the reason why. The beast might have a flawed eye or its brain might have been damaged at birth. Whatever the cause, the flaw was slight but ominous. When he ran up against the lance, Glitsch was steady and true. But when the opposing lance-tip came within a meter of his head, Glitsch shied to the right. Never to the left, never more than a few centimeters, but he always shied and always to the right. Any good jouster would notice that by round two or three, and tafpa jousts went for five rounds. Glitsch's rider would surely lose the match once his opponent made that discovery.

Jan leaned forward again and patted the beast between the oval-shaped ears. Even there the pelt was moist. The workout had lasted hours. "Poor Glitsch," he said aloud. "Poor, dear Glitsch." He scratched the tafpa at the base of the left ear. "You'll never be a jouster, that's for sure. I'll have to tell Sondus that you'll be a racer instead. What a shame, old buddy. The son of Frotsch a racer. How you disgrace your line. But it's no use pretending any longer."

He hadn't told anyone about Glitsch's flaw. He had pretended and pretended. To think that Jan Rigg couldn't fix a little thing like lance-shyness in a tafpa. He was too good a tafchuko to admit that. At twenty-five he was still young, of course. The best tafchukos were in their thrities. But age counted for much less than "feel," and "feel" he had a-plenty.

All the Riggs had the feel. For three generations the headman of Potsla Run had been a Rigg. Jan had no hopes of ending as a headman. He was too hot-headed for that. A headman had to suck up to the Castle lords. Jan refused to do that and had been chided for it. Sondus, his father, always said to him, "It's not year 1, you know. It's 873. We're not the early settlers any more. This is the modern age. We must bend with circumstances. You're too romantic and too stubborn for your own good." No; Jan didn't have his father's cool steadiness. He wouldn't be headman, but one of his brothers would surely be chosen. Old Jaimo Potsla would make sure that another Rigg replaced the old man when the time came.

But no doubt about it. He was a good tafchuko and it hurt him to have failed with Glitsch. Sondus would be furious. As a jouster Glitsch would fetch ten thousand credits at the auction. As a racer he was worth three or four at best. But he could not pretend that Glitsch had the makings of a jouster. Potsla's reputation was at stake. Potsla tafpas were the finest: the racers swift, the jousters gutsy. They never shied, not even a millimeter. Jan had tried to fix that shying since early Spring. He had failed and guessed now that it couldn't be done.

He lifted the lance tip off the turf and nudged Glitsch into motion. They crossed the field wobbling past the empty bleachers. Jan's thoughts darkened. He recalled lords seated on those benches in robes of silver and of gold sipping tea through colored straws, pointing at the tafpas on display with jeweled fingers . . . He spat on the ground, soul-sore that he had to serve the lords. He loved his tafchuko life, had known no other, but it burned his manhood to know himself "protected" while Sophie was exposed.

Sophie, sweet Sophie. He planned to slip away tonight to see her at Simalta—Siege or not, tundrati or not, his father's scowling neither here nor there. Sondus disapproved of Sophie. She was a city girl and a Tessori to boot. Sondus scorned the Tesso cult and what he called their "weird and pale-ass ways." But Jan loved Sophie and defied his father. Days had passed since he had seen her and she had acted oddly on the visiphone. She tried to hide something, but he knew her too well to be taken in.

Sudden apprehension chilled him. The Siege had come. She *was* exposed. Concession's computers had her name and photograph. She too might be summoned like all those other hundreds, thousands, year in year out.

God save us, he thought. He carried a lox ear around his neck on a string, and now he reached up to touch it for luck. "It'll be all right again this year," he said aloud, addressing Glitsch. "She'll be all right." He pushed out of mind any thought of what he might do if she *were* summoned.

He guided Glitsch between two dummies at the end of the field. They had spent the afternoon running up against the dummies in the volta. His arm was so tired, he thought it would fall off. He had held the training lance under his armpit and had spurred Glitsch against the dummies. Each dummy had a swivelled lance attached to its frame. He had slapped the lance aside time and again and had sunk his own lance into the bale of straw that represented the opposing jouster. He had tried to hold Glitsch absolutely steady and on target. But his buddy had shied, and shied.

He took off his soft, floppy hat and wiped his face with it. They reached the road and headed for the stables. To his right, through Nary pines, he could see a white shimmering from the guest houses. The ride jarred his spine. At a slow walk tafpa riding had a painfully rocky feel. Jan bounced up and down and sideways. During the volta tafpa legs carried you like a bird. Walking a tafpa felt like running on stilts nailed to your shoulder blades. Up ahead the lights of the mansion beckoned, blinking through foilage. The breeze carried a scent of bangor. Behind the mansion, at the headman's house, dinner waited. He was hungry. But before he ate he had to hike back up to the hunting lodge to feed the felina and the lox. He had promised sick Ricardo's wife to do this. It was a long way to the stables and a long way back, but he didn't have the heart to spur Glitsch into the volta again. By the acrid smell of the beast, its humps were pumped empty of hormone.

Some time later he arrived at the hunting lodge. In the dark, fenced enclosure next to the lodge, felina and lox stirred restlessly in cages. Jan saw phosphorescent eyes glow in the darkness, yellowish felina eyes, green lox eyes. Cold and hungry eyes. He smelled urine and meat-breath. Somewhere in a nearby tree Lura-lura began her throaty song: "Tru-root, tru-root, tru-ree-root." He took a bucket of cut-up baguse meat and began to feed the spotted cats. They growled and purred in the darkness as they fell to eating.

Halfway through this chore, Jan heard the loudspeaker's crackle from a corner of the hunting lodge. The switchboard operator paged him.

He found a rag and wiped his hands before he went into the lodge to take the call.

The caller was Maria. The moment he saw her serious mien in the tiny screen, he knew something was wrong. His guts grew tight; he thought of Sophie. Maria was a teacher of the Will, supremely schooled in moral culture, and she had herself under control—too much so, Jan thought.

"It's about Sophie," he said, out of breath. His body pulsed with unnatural excitement. His glands spilled hormones—like the humps of a voltating tafpa.

He listened to her story in silence, staring at the tiny screen. His heart was racing but he took in the facts without external reaction. Sophie had been summoned.

She had already gone to the Tower. She had asked Maria to tell Jan after her departure.

He understood Sophie's intentions. If anyone in the world could, Maria could give him this message in the calmest and most rational way.

Sophie had been mature about it, Maria said. She had left in good spirits. She had urged Jan to rise above himself, to rise above the situation, to keep his head.

"It's your nature to act precipitously, Jan," Maria said. "Sophie was afraid of that. If you want to honor her wishes, you won't do anything foolish."

"Thank you, Maria," he said. Emotions choked his voice into a whisper. "Thanks for calling." He punched off the visiphone and walked out of the lodge as if in a daze.

He stood for a moment oblivious of the animals' growling and Lura-lura's throaty calling. A dark, gloomy blackness opened up inside him and told him what to do. He took the lox-ear from around his neck and tossed it into the darkness. Then slowly, calmly, he left the hill and headed toward the mansion.

He took the back way—pebbled paths winding amidst aromatic gardens each with its fountain and trellised gazebo. He crossed the circle formed by the guest houses, now empty. He approached the mansion complex from the back and entered Farod's hut, the saddler's shop. There he quickly found a wall rack with leather cutting knives. He chose a round-handled implement with a wide blade that curved into a sharp point and stuck it blade-first into his right boot.

Some time later he could be seen walking toward Simalta along Sarto road. In the distance tall buildings reflected a random scattering of light. He stared fixedly at one of these, the Tower of Faltara. His aim tonight was very simple. He would barge into that building and he would find her. Then he would bring her out again. Or else he would die tonight, trying to save her. He saw no other alternative, and it made him quite cheerful.

He reached Simalta's outskirts by ten o'clock, the Tower half an hour later. The Tower faced a small park ringed with trees. Jan entered the park and sat down on a bench. From there he observed the building's main entry—a winged door above three flights of wide, marble stairs. He waited patiently watching a few visitors come and go. A few fompa came, lifting their robes as they mounted the steps. A few fompa left and drove off in floaters. Most of those who came and went were tundrati, both officers and men. Jan waited until all movement died, then he waited even longer. One yellow floater still hung before the building. A tundratus colonel had left it there some time ago. The colonel had not emerged. Jan waited yet a little longer; then he decided that the time had come. He reached down for Farod's knife and set off toward the Tower.

6 — SERENDIPITY IN THE TOWER

On August 27 (September 2, System reckoning) the challenge was presented to the Contortus family. This was the earliest possible date in that Balto Fangano required time to secure the total commitment of his family and to integrate the family's planning with that of Cush at the staff level.

Soon thereafter the services of a tafpa expert were secured. We had the erroneous impression at the time that superiority in tafpa jousting was an important element of success.

Serendipitously, and unbeknownst to anyone in the leadership circle, a female agent was recruited at the same time by a district coordinator. Her contributions would later be of greater significance than those of the tafchuko, although the two cases were closely linked.

—Ronald Frederick, Report to the
23rd Subplenum of the Centennial
Party Central Committee.

Mart stepped into the levitator and punched the button for the ground floor. The doors slid shut, the levitator dropped. He closed his eyes and sighed. Exhausted. He had visited all thirteen herb shops, had talked to Fompus Richter. Elements of that discussion

still cluttered his mind. Too much risk, he thought. Too
damned much risk . . .

He had plotted with the fompus about the island of
Gash. Gash held the Concession's military power—
four thousand trained tundrati slaves. Gash had to be
neutralized during the crucial days, but to paralyze the
island, Mart needed help from his supporters among the
military on Riondi. Only a space scout could arrive on
Gash fast enough to score a surprise.

The trouble is, Mart thought, I have to get to Riondi
somehow to make arrangements with Colonel Robartus. You can't do things like that by message—or even
messenger.

But to travel to Riondi . . . that meant a trip out into
Space. And once in Space, even if he could somehow
get there, didn't he have an obligation to abscond?
Conflicting loyalties . . .

Enough, Mart thought. Enough work for one day.
He rubbed his eyes, stretched, yawned. Time to shed
this ridiculous tundratus uniform, then sleep. He
longed for sleep. Too late to find a room, especially
during the Siege, but he would park his floater in a
secluded spot and curl up in the back. Rested and more
lucky, he would find the tafchuko tomorrow.

The levitator stopped, doors slid aside. In the
Tower's office wing all was deathly still. In the other
wing, floor after floor would be filled with slaves in
tape-sleep. All that would end soon, God willing . . .

He stepped from the levitator and took a course
toward the lobby. Lights shone in the tiles of the long
and empty corridor. His boots clacked eerily, raising
echoes. He marched in tundratus disguise complete
with boots, breeches, and a shima-feathered hat. To
avoid any unpleasentness at the door, he had donned a
colonel's jacket. Tundrati colonels intimidated com-

mon soldiers. The guards hadn't even asked to see his
ID chit. Menoma had its useful aspects.

As he approached the lobby, he heard the muffled
sounds of a commotion—cries, dull blows, groans, and
the sound of running. Mart hesitated for a moment.
Should he go on? He could become embroiled in need-
less trouble. Cush doctrine demanded control of conflict situations. Never let the other guy take the initiative. Never react. Never let the enemy select the
battleground. In this instance he went on, trusting in his
uniform. But he moved on tip-toes. And when he came
to the last corner, he peered around it first.

Several tundrati stood in a bunch, arms and legs
flailing. They beat and kicked a person Mart couldn't
see—not even in the reflection of the large double-
winged door. One tundratus stood outside the flailing,
grunting circle. He leaned against the wall, bent over,
his face a grimmace of pain. Blood dripped from the
slashed sleeve of his tunic and spattered on the white-
green marble floor.

Mart stepped forward and the wounded soldier saw
him. Conditioning overcame the soldier's trauma, and
with a flicker of anxiety in his dull eyes he stood up.
"Officer!" he yelled. "Attention!"

The small clump of tundrati immediately broke
apart. The soldiers came to attention facing the colonel.
As they parted, they revealed a slender young man
dressed—

No question about it! A young tafchuko. He wore a
ruffled white shirt, blue breeches, and black boots. The
boots showed the white markings left by salty tafpa
sweat. On the floor near him lay a floppy tafchuko hat.
Next to the hat lay a bloody, round-handled saddler's
knife. That knife, presumably, had wounded the tundratus.

Oh, Great Serendipity, Mart thought. You've sent me a tafchuko. Now, of all times. Now when I can only think of sleep.

The tafchuko looked at Mart through uncomprehending eyes, his face cut up and blotched. He swayed on unsteady legs. Presently his knees buckled and he collapsed on the floor.

"Who's in charge? Report!" Mart barked. He wished he knew the "deep command" to which these men responded. If he knew it, he could order them to forget what they had seen.

His eyes found the senior guard; the man stepped forward, stamped his boots, saluted. Mart nodded repeatedly as the soldier told his story in halting sentences. This man—a finger pointed to the heap on the marble—had tried to force his way into the Tower. He had threatened with a knife. He said he wanted his girl. He had cut up Globus, here. Globus had yelled for help and they had come to subdue the intruder.

The subject of the conversation lay sprawled on the marble floor, unconscious. Mart had arrived in the nick of time. Another five minutes and the man would have been dead.

He interrupted the guard's report. Light streamed from an open office down another corridor. The sergeant of the guard would be asleep in there, probably full of cicillo. Asleep or not, Mart didn't want to take any chances. Sergeants had longer memories than common soldiers. They might question strange colonels who appeared out of nowhere.

"I'll take this character to Ferrari barracks with me," he announced to the senior guard. "My floater is outside. Carry him out and bring his gear."

He marched to the door resolutely without turning back. The Conditioning could be trusted, even if he didn't use the deep command. Tundrati memories were woefully short and consequently these men were not suspicious types, not in these early years of service.

He went down three flights of marble stairs. The street lay deserted; the little park in front of the Tower loomed dark. He stopped by the floater and turned about to observe. Four tundrati brought the tafchuko, two holding his arms, two his legs. The senior guard tagged along behind carrying the young man's hat and knife.

In the darkness Mart smiled to himself. Concession itself delivered the tafchuko he had come to recruit. Balto had been right this morning. The man had dropped into his lap.

PART II

7 — MEETINGS ON DOMINUS

His face suddenly overran with purple from real or pretended rage; then Captain Brudd moved forward from the edge of the Fangano riding hall waving an arm.

"No, no, no," he shouted. "Stop. That's no way to charge the dummy, you stupid imbecile. Get off that beast before I kick you off."

The oval riding hall lay bathed in light from a tinted, milky dome of glass. Jousting dummies made of straw hulked against one end, their lances at the ready. Stable boys squatted behind them near a pyramid of hay amusing themselves with dice. Two tafpas on the far side of the hall stirred up the greenish sawdust under the direction of mediocre riders. In the center snorted Snoorok, his humps a-steam with hormones. Heavyset, shy Fillip slid off Snoorok's back. Holding the tafpa's bridle, he bent his head obediently while Brudd sputtered and fulminated in growing waves of fury.

Fat Fillip happened to be Jan's best friend up here on Dominus—and Captain Brudd's favorite whipping boy. Jan watched the scene. He leaned against the waist-high wall of a vaulted arcade that ran around the hall. His hands were balled in fists; his eyes gleamed with anger. He had the urge to interfere but didn't dare to do it. Tough weeks of training had transformed him into a man of Cush and hence into a man of discipline. He followed his instructions to the letter.

Keep your mouth shut, he told himself. Don't make a scene.

Treat the Captain as your boss; don't ask any questions; don't be surprised by anything you see—no matter how strange. You will learn the background soon enough.

How soon? Jan wondered. Everything that he had seen up here had made him wonder. He liked Fillip very much, for instance; he guessed that the fat boy was a member of the Movement too, assigned to the Fanganos to help with the revolution. But Fillip had been sent to train the tafpas, and Fillip was no tafchuko and never would be one.

And Captain Brudd? Captain Brudd a tafpa-master? The captain had no "feel" at all. Why did Balto and his fompus let the captain brutalize the stable staff? Balto was a kindly person who smiled a lot and always had nice words to say to everyone. The fompus, Leo, seemed to be a decent man as well despite his evident reserve and the far-away look in his eyes. Captain Brudd didn't fit this household.

Penta Mart had told Jan very little about the Fangano family. "One thing at a time," he'd said. "We have three weeks to turn you into a Cushman, and you have much to learn, my friend. Concentrate on training. Discipline your curiosity." So Jan had settled down to train in a small and hidden camp north of Simalta. He learned a lot about the trade of revolution—and about himself—and almost nothing about his assignment. "Later," Penta always said. "Right now you have no need to know."

He had arrived up here a week ago—by way of the Tower and Castle's airport. With other tundrati he had been herded down into Level Three and held in pens that animals would have found confining. One night a Cush supporter had found him and helped him escape to the surface. He had found the Fangano palace in no time at all. The password had earned him admittance and an interview with Balto—but the Fangano chief said as little as Penta Mart. He urged Jan to obey the captain and to wonder at nothing else. So Jan obeyed the captain. But it took real effort.

Brudd was a big and heavy man with purple skin and crazy eyes. The eyes turned tiny when he indulged his temper, as he did now—shouting and flailing with his riding crop in such a fury that Snoorok reared and tugged madly at Fillip's hand. Fillip endured it all with a passive stolid expression. Did he have orders to obey the captain too?

What a beast, that Brudd—violent, drunken, and tyrannical. He used the men as if they were his property. By day he bullied and insulted them, by night he dragged them to cheap taverns down on Level Three where slaves endured a dreadful squalor and the stench of levitron took your breath away. Brudd didn't like to be alone.

Unlike the others, Jan liked these excursions. He looked for Sophie everywhere. She wouldn't be the Sophie he had known and wouldn't recognize him, but he longed to see her anyway. Someday he would rescue her and teach her who she really was. She would learn to love him as in the days gone by . . .

He watched Brudd, Fillip, and jumpy, nervous Snoorok. Two other trainers had brought their beasts to volta and attacked the dummies clumsily. They rushed forward, lances high, and drove the training weapons into bales of straw.

All of this struck Jan as just a little too playful. The

riding hall—too short for serious training; a voltating tafpa couldn't reach top speed in here. The trainers knew nothing about jousting, and the tafpas lacked all talent. Potsla Run would have been ashamed to *give* such nags away. Balto seldom came. He had potential as a jouster; he had a remarkably steady seat. But Balto seemed to behave with deliberate clumsiness and relied on Brudd for all advice. Jan had tried to help the chief on one occasion and had been gruffly rebuffed.

Jan relaxed his face as Brudd turned from Fillip at last and came back Jan's way. Brudd never picked on Jan. Sometimes their eyes had crossed in moments of tension, and the captain had always yielded first—revealing an inner softness. Nonetheless, Jan always tried to be the perfect subordinate.

Brudd came—a slack expression on his ruddy face. He seemed to have spent his rage and now looked more stupid than mean.

"Jan," he said, "take over for me. I have to run an errand." A ghost of his earlier rage crossed his face. "Make the imbecile *drive* that animal!"

"Will do," Jan said. He pushed himself away from the wall, and the captain passed into the palace through a vaulted door.

Captain Brudd left the Fangano palace by a side entrance and walked with exaggerated aimlessness in the direction of Central Square. The Fangano complex occupied modest acreage on one of the inner circumferentials reserved for minor families. Brudd made for the nearest Diagonal leading to the center, to the capitol; the white, domed structure with columns all around could be seen in the distance. A golden statue with an outstretched hand gleamed in the sun on top of the capitol.

An agent of the Fangano household, dressed like a senior procurement slave and assigned to keep track of Brudd's movements, found it playfully easy to follow Brudd. He avoided detection easily when the captain—his face as red as his tundratus tunic, the white shima-feather in his hat moving in the breeze—peered back suspiciously from time to time.

The streets of Dominus stood virtually empty—elaborately carved stone housefronts facing colorful, tiled walks. Most of the households had already moved down to the Fair Grounds in South Bosom in preparation for the games. Staffs labored down there in Tent City. Lords and ladies gamboled on the beaches under tundratus protection; or sailed the ocean; or hunted and fished. Skeleton staffs remained on Dominus—complements of guards to protect the buildings against vandalism, a few slaves, and one or two junior fompa to run the show. Most of the slaves passing Brudd worked for Central Administration. Their badges identified them as servants of Maintenance, Streets, Power, Transportation, Procurement, and similar departments. A few tundrati of the Castle Reserve saluted the captain; he returned these greetings with sloppy movements of his hand. Brudd was out of sorts.

Once arrived at Central Square, he ducked into a squalid bar under the arcade around the flagstoned open space encircling the capitol. He ordered and gulped three tall glasses of green cicillo.

He needed fortification to face that man Drusilla. The fompus caused Brudd plenty of pain. Drusilla hungered for information and never could be satisfied. Brudd's reporting time had come and yet he had no news to bring. The Contortus family had moved to Faltara days ago. Drusilla had stayed behind to give Brudd more time to nose about. Drusilla planned to leave tonight—and Brudd had still not "produced."

Emboldened by alcohol, Brudd made straight for the Contortus palace along Ignazio Boulevard, the Diagonal connecting the Capitol with East Corner. He didn't care whether he was seen or not.

Contortus Palace was the Castle's largest single structure. It occupied an entire corner of the levitating city. Drusilla had enlarged the palace eight years ago to celebrate the family's accession to virtually undisputed rule; he had built sixteen new towers because Ignazio had been sixteen that year, the youngest Controller of Tundrati in Fillippi's history and already famous as the invincible dueller, Ignazio "Seven Lives" Contortus.

A massive wall encircled the palace topped with small towers of its own. A guard opened the heavy, creaky door; he wore a tundratus uniform with the "leaping felina" on his lapel—emblem of the Contortus family.

Huffing a little from his walk, busy inventing excuses for his failure to "produce," Brudd hurried toward North Wing and Drusilla's offices. He kept his eyes on the checkered floor of the corridor—huge squares of black and gold—but he looked up to nod at guards spaced at intervals. Most of these men had served with him before.

A clerk with shaved head told Brudd to wait in an outer office. Drusilla's clerks aped their master; they shaved their heads and spoke in icy tones. Brudd sat morosely and stared at a huge photograph of Ignazio Contortus—the pudgy face, that hairdo with the central streak. The clerk called at last.

Drusilla sat erect behind a desk in an office of almost excessive order: all here was rectangularity, from the papers on the desk to the charts on the wall. Drusilla let Brudd stand. He stared at the captain. "Well?" he said.

Brudd's eyes darted about the office as if searching for devices of torture. Instead he saw stiff chairs around a table, black communications boxes, and a red vis-iphone that linked Drusilla to the island of Gash. Large charts on hooks covered most walls. Brudd dropped his eyes.

"Nothing much happened this week, fompus." He cringed inwardly, anticipating a blow. "Business as usual. Balto came to work out again. He looked as clumsy as ever. The rest of the time we trained. Leo insists that we train fourteen hours a day. That leaves very little time for anything else."

He looked up to see Drusilla's reaction. From the bronze-colored bald head Drusilla's eyes stared back at him like pieces of polished steel.

Drusilla regarded the bloated drunkard and wrinkled his nose at the reek of cicillo. He controlled his fury well. The imbecile had not produced, the red-faced lush lacked competence. Drusilla had delayed his trip to wait for this . . . this piggish has-been of a captain! Solumnos Teck was already down there—no doubt agitating. Teck had complained in strident tones saying that Brudd was less than useless. He called for drastic measures. Trouble was—Sol Teck was right!

"You're not worth two hundred credits a week," Drusilla said at last. "You're not worth a single credit, Brudd. I ought to ship you back to Riondi—as a sergeant."

Brudd winced at the thought. Riondi was hell. A vision of the dusty planet flashed into his mind: the endless bombardment; the crowded, hot life under-crust; guard duty at night topside in the howling *furcsa* where sand beat against your goggles and you couldn't see the sensor gauges for the life of you; the diveplanes heading for the water mains; thirst.

"I'm doing the best I can," he said. "I swear it. I'm new in the household. Nobody trusts me yet. Give me time."

"You've had weeks, Brudd, weeks. Four weeks. And you haven't produced a damn thing."

Brudd didn't answer. He simply waited for the next blow. The air trembled with tension; Drusilla stared. At last he spoke:

"Well, what about the Potsla auction. Are you going to that?"

Brudd nodded. "Balto is going."

"You mean you're not?"

Brudd swallowed. Lying to this fompus had its hazards. Damn his eyes, he thought, damn this man.

"He's taking one of the trainers with him, but I was told to stay and intensify the work."

"Stay? Where? Here on Dominus? You are to stay up here? All the world is on Faltara! When are you scheduled to move? You must know that, at least."

"No schedule has been announced yet."

Another long silence. Drusilla radiated an immense rage but showed no sign of it except in the eyes. Nevertheless Brudd found himself enveloped in the man's fury and wanted to get out of there. Once well down the hall, he could forget about this bald menace with the steely eyes—until the next time.

"Very well, Brudd," the fompus said at last. "I told you the last time and I am telling you now, for the *very* last time: produce or I will have your hide. Right here."

Drusilla made a gesture of smoothing out a wrinkled pelt over the desk top. "The moment you people get down to the island, I want to see you in my tent. You better have some information—enough to make a plan. If you fail me once more, Brudd, it will be the end of you."

He lifted a hand and gestured Brudd away—the

gesture of a man shooing a fly. He turned back to his papers, thinking that he would have to invent some information to counter Sol Teck's whisperings. Everything went rockily at present, rockily, most rockily.

Brudd walked down the checkered corridor, his lips moving silently. He cursed Drusilla back there in that silver robe. Produce . . .! Produce what? Produce how? The devil himself would have a time of it with those strange Fanganos. Nobody seemed to use the deep command to keep the slaves in line. The slaves acted oddly—as if they had never touched Menoma. A peculiarly friendly atmosphere prevailed in that place, but Brudd had no share in it. Voices fell silent when he appeared. Nobody spoke to him. All seemed ignorant of the fact that Balto would have to fight a blood-joust a mere three weeks from now. He had found no friends or confidantes. He hadn't even found a girl. How could he get the facts when no one talked to—His rushing thoughts were cut off abruptly. Mistress Sultana turned a corner just ahead. He knew the woman from way back—she managed the palace entertainers. Sultana stopped to curtsy—a cowled, robed matron with a sharp nose and penetrating, worldly eyes. Numerous golden rings jangled in her ears and around her skinny arms. Three shaven slave girls had knelt down behind her. They carried musical instruments.

Sultana brought fond memories. She had been a friend of Brudd's during his days as a guard lieutenant in the palace. From time to time when conditions had been right, and for a small consideration, she had allowed her girls to entertain him in those days.

"Sultana!" he cried, his voice cheery with pleasant surprise. "Are you still here? I thought the household had gone to the island."

She looked at him through calculating eyes. "Not

this time, Captain. For reasons that are unclear to me, they left us behind." Her tone revealed resentment toward unnamed superiors.

"Well . . ." he said. "I expect that you'll be bored . . . and ready for a little company, eh?" Lest she mistake his intentions he leered and pinched her skinny hip.

She cackled a little and jerked away from him.

"Drusilla leaves tonight," she said. Her voice had a reedy quality. "But tomorrow!!!"

"Don't be surprised if I drop in," he said, and winked. "I'll bring along a friend or two, if you don't mind." He leaned toward her, pinched her cheek. "One will be just for you, my dear, a young, strong boy."

"That might be fun," she said, and smiled. Then she placed a hand on his arm. "But tell me. What brings you back to our fair planet. Isn't your return a little . . . premature?"

His face turned serious. "That's a little hush-hush, my dear. Drusilla and I—we're on a little project together. We might chat about that tomorrow just a bit, the two of us. Do you still stock Tinarrian schnapps?"

"Only the very best for my close friends," she fluted.

"Tomorrow, then." He gave her a mock salute, she curtsied with a jangle of rings, then he continued on his way toward the discrete entry where he had come in; his mood was much improved. His next meeting with Drusilla was still sometime in the future. And by then, perhaps, he might even have some information.

In the Fangano riding hall, Jan sat high on Snoorok and demonstrated various proper lance positions to Fillip and the other so-called trainers. It pleased him to have a chance to show his skills, and the young men clearly enjoyed the lesson. A clerk then entered the riding hall. He stood a moment on the riding oval's edge. Then he made a beckoning gesture to Jan.

A moment later Jan learned that Fompus Leo wished to see him. He brushed his clothing and arranged his hair. Then he followed the clerk into the palace feeling the stir of excitement. Perhaps now he would learn a little about his assignment.

They passed cheerful murals on the way—scenes from Felicitas, ancestral home of the Fanganos back in New Frontier. It was a heavy planet full of solid, bulky animals and plants. The beasts resembled the marsupial classification. Jan found them droll but lovable. All the plants were thick of stem and wide of leaf. Through windows on one side of the corridor he could see some of the same plants. Harom Fangano, Balto's uncle, tried to grow them in a garden and produced monstrosities. In Fillippi's gravity, Felicitas vegetation luxuriated into the vertical with absurd vengeance.

Fompus Leo, usually so distant and unapproachable, received Jan with kind words and led him into a colorful, dark room. Mandala-shaped rubayat rugs hung on the wall; their phosphorescent fibers caused a rich glow of color against black backgrounds. Leather-covered armchairs and couches stood around a bubbling fountain lighted from beneath. Against a wall stood a carved table filled with precious glow-rocks from New Frontier.

Leo wore embroidered slippers, a silver robe; a huge green turban graced his head. His beard was black and bushy, his lips and nose youthfully red. Nonetheless, the heavy lines on his brow and the wrinkled, spotted skin of the hand he had stretched out in greeting revealed a man well past his middle years.

He asked Jan to sit and sank into a chair himself. The fountain warbled between them. The fompus crossed his legs and asked Jan how he liked it here. Did he like his room, the food? Felicitas fare, Felicitas spices might not appeal to a Fillippi palate. As Jan responded, Leo slowly stroked his beard.

After some of these preliminaries, Leo changed the tone slightly: "You've made a good impression here," he said. "Balto has a very high opinion of you. You're an asset to our household even if we haven't used your talents yet. But that'll come. Penta Mart has chosen well. But we knew he would. Tell me, Jan, how did you pass the Menoma gauntlet and the tundratus conditioning? None the worse for it, I hope?"

He saw Jan hesitating, said: "All of us in the Fangano household are part of the conspiracy. You can relax. But just to set you at your ease, the password is 'east gate.'"

"Yes, sir," Jan said. 'I had no trouble in the Tower. The drug made me ill, but other than that it had no effect. I had a tough time at first, but Olaf got me out of there in four days. While it lasted I thought I'd die of lack of sleep."

"The tapes?"

"Yes. They had me in kinesthetic machines all day long—learning to walk and move again." Jan shook his head wonderingly. "Then all night long on tapes learning to speak and all that. And all the time I had to be on guard not to let on that I was conscious."

The green turban nodded, the hand stroked the beard.

"And all this after two weeks of the worst kind of drill and cramming I had ever had."

Leo smiled and raised his eyebrows: "Delivered to Penta's tender mercies?"

Jan chuckled, nodded. "Yes. I don't know what's worse—having pictures of Ignazio flashed at you hour after hour and hearing his leadership praised—or having hand-to-hand combat practice with Penta Mart. I wished myself back on Potsla Run many a time in those days."

Leo smiled. "Among other things I've called you in to talk about Potsla Run. As it stands now, you'll be going back there for a visit very shortly. Do you see any problem in that?"

Jan's heart jumped. How he longed to see the Run again. Then he frowned. "I'm sure to be recognized."

"That's no problem. You'll be wearing a disguise—a beard, a wig, and fompus robes."

"Am I going to the auction?"

Leo nodded. "Yes, we have to buy a top-notch animal for the joust, and Potsla is the place to get one, as I'm sure you'll agree. Is it true that you know every tafpa on the ranch?"

"Not every tafpa, but . . ."

"Good. You'll go with Balto. Your job will be to help him pick the best tafpa on the ranch. Money is no object. The Contorti will be down there bidding against us. I'd like to go myself, but our mutual friend has imposed a small chore on me during the auction."

In spirit Jan was already back on Potsla Run. The fompus in his leather armchair, legs crossed under the silver robe, the carved table filled with oddly shaped mementoes made of glowing crystal, the hypontic rubayat rugs—all this was illusion. Potsla Run was real.

He thought of the jousting tafpas on the Run. Glitsch would be best of all, if only he didn't shy. The Run wouldn't even offer him for sale as a jouster. That left a wide selection . . .

"I know exactly the beast we need," he said. "It's Fleatcher, probably the best jouster on the Run."

"When you get down there, young man, you'd better hide your enthusiasm," Leo said. "We don't want Drusilla bidding him away. Or is it a *her?*"

Jan smiled in embarrassment. Like the rest of the Fangano household, Leo knew little about tafpas. "Tafpas are neither—or, I mean, they are both. Male and female," Jan said. "They mate by rubbing their humps together. But we always say 'he' when we talk about a tafpa."

The fompus smiled. "He or she," he said, "you must be very careful. Be guided by Balto, and do as he says. Above all, you must control yourself—no matter what happens and who you may see. Penta says that you are rash—but he says that you have matured a little under his not-so-gentle care."

Jan looked down. He recalled his suicidal caper at the Tower. He recalled, as well, his tantrums after his rescue—wishing to die, unwilling to live with Sophie a Menoma slave. Only slowly had Penta's arguments brought him around to reason—and later to participation in the Movement. The pain of those days had now been overlaid by a healing scar of learning, new experience, and hope. He would find Sophie. He felt it in his guts.

"You must be reformed." Leo continued. "You've obeyed us to the letter—regarding Captain Brudd. You must have guessed by now that he isn't one of us. He is a Contortus spy."

"Oh," Jan said. "But . . ."

"We thought it best to let them place an agent in the household, one we knew to be an agent from the start. But you needn't worry. Brudd hasn't learned a thing.

And before we go down to the island, we will lock him up here. But in the meantime, carry on as usual.''

Leo stood up. He led Jan to the door with a fatherly arm around the young man's shoulder.

''You go to Potsla Run the day after tomorrow,'' he said. ''Your disguise will be waiting for you in the chopper.''

''May I ask some questions?''

''No,'' Leo said, at the door. ''Let's just take one step at a time.''

8 — A BRIEFING ON RIONDI

The scout ship left a so-called "short-horned" time-collapse tunnel and broke out of TC in orbit around Riondi. Mart saw the planet in his screen—a dense, red ball a-swirl with tan-colored, dusty weather systems. Riondi was a dreadful world, essentially useless for everything except warfare. By unstated agreement, Empire and System waged war for the planet as a proxy for Fillippi. Whoever ended up in control here would possess the flower planet. The war had been fought for eighty years without issue—and would be fought for eighty more, Mart guessed. The Riondi war—he was still too high up to see any signs of it below—resembled a hundred similiar skirmishes all over Outermost; only a few were decided every fifty years or so.

The young pilot, seated in the center of the saucer in a rotating chair, came around to face Mart. "Are you ready?" Mart nodded. "Here we go," the pilot said, swivelling again. "Hold on to your britches." Then he engaged the saucer's rotor jets, turned the ship on edge, and the craft sliced its way into Riondi's atmosphere.

Mart wondered how he would explain all this to the commissars back home—one of these days. The young pilot was no match for an agent of his skill and experience. A quick lunge and a single chop—then Mart would be the master of a System Scout Ship Model V—the latest and most potent addition to the System fleet for both offensive and defensive purposes. Those commissars who would some day try him had sent him to Pappacappolous for no other reason than to steal the *plans* for such a babe as this. He could bring them the whole vessel; he had observed the pilot closely in Fillippi's atmosphere and then in space—both entering and leaving time-collapse. He could operate the craft.

A lunge, a chop—and he'd be on his way to the nearest Empire planet. Hondo Thackus would be foiled and Ronald Frederick vindicated.

But Mart couldn't get himself to do it. He could not betray his friends or abandon the people of Fillippi in their finest hour. Hell, he thought, it's worse than that. I can't stand the thought of an unfinished job.

And, he thought, in the end I'll end up with one of these babies yet—Drusilla's saucer.

The tiny ship dropped down over the southern pole—a sickly mound of ice. Then it skittered and slid at low altitudes over the cratered mass of the desolate planet at speeds well beyond the speed of sound. Mart marvelled at the craft. He had seen films of it many years ago but had never been an occupant in such a wonder-craft. It seemed to take a random path aimed toward the southern Rim Sea—more or less. Magnet-seeking booby bombs exploded by the hundreds in its wake over a distance of a thousand kilometers—their wondrous mushrooms coming and going in Mart's screen—and not a one so much as grazed the vessel's hull. What amazing shields it had, the Scout Ship Model V. Mart's fingers itched to handle the controls.

Suddenly the craft tilted on edge again and plunged into the thick, briny soup of the sea. Mines exploded all about and the vibrations rocked but failed to damage the

scout. It wobbled slowly toward the subsurface dock-
ing station located two thousand meters under the crust
and settled gently into a lock.

Mart left the ship by way of a rubber tube-way that
had attached itself to the saucer's underside. Arms out
to steady himself, he walked as in a net. A delegation of
officers waited in a small reception cave. A quick round
of handshakes—then the group made for a nearby con-
ference room.

As they hastened down the narrow hall, Mart saw
through windows on both sides soldiers asleep over
communications instruments, at weapons panels, at
desks. Men loyal to the Movement manned critical
stations; each man held a drug-gun at the ready in case
anyone awakened. Colonel Robartus and his boys had
put this outpost under drug—no mean maneuver in
itself. The sleeping victims of the gun had angelic
expressions; they slept deeply.

Mart composed his thoughts. He had very little time.
The menomic drug worked for thirty minutes. If he
could leave before that time, all the sleepers would
awaken without memory of having slept, without a
sense of lapsed time. If he overstayed his welcome and
a second dose had to be shot, the sleepers would
awaken and remember something. That might raise
questions and create a risk.

They entered the room—a plain cavity cut from
bedrock, roughly, with a plasma torch. Molten rock
covered the walls like poorly spread paint.

They settled around a plain, grey, functional table.
The room was hot—hot enough so that the men unzipped their tunics. Colonel Tussalla Robartus took one
end of the table, inviting Mart to take the other. Then
the colonel kicked off the meeting.

Robartus was a blondish, square-jawed, bulb-nosed,

long-limbed man—the first officer Mart had ever re-cruited. Robartus had gathered the rest of these men—all veterans of the Polar Camp, all System officers now but Cushmen first and last. Robartus scratched a hook-shaped scar on his left cheek; his eyes twinkled with excitement but his heavily-lined features were grave.

"I talked to the group briefly before you arrived, Penta," he began, "and I told them why you were coming. All of us are Cushmen. We are ready to deliver on our commitment to the Movement. We knew it would come, sooner or later. I guess the time is now."

Mart nodded his head slowly, looked down at the table top.

"I appreciate what you have done. Bringing me here was risky enough. And the people of Fillippi will re-member what you will do for them." He looked up. "As you know," he went on, "I didn't want to involve those of you serving on Riondi. Those of us back home have a lot to lose if things go wrong, but you have more to lose. You are in the service and at war, and if you are to help me, you will have to leave your posts. I wish I could find some other way—but there seems to be no other. I have come to ask you to risk being shot as deserters."

"Don't waste time," Robartus said. "We have been over all of that and we are ready to pay the price." Then a sudden smile crossed his face. "We're not so sure that the Administration will deal harshly with us for 'help-ing' just a little."

Mart smiled back. "I hope so too. But you never know. Let's get down to the issue. Under the Conces-sion's constitution, as you know, if our man defeats Ignazio in the up-coming duel, he becomes general of the tundrati and thus the effective power on the island. Back when you and I started, Tuss—" Mart glanced at

Robartus ''—I was sure that we could win simply by winning on the jousting field. But lately I have come to change my mind.''

''Why? Don't you think Drusilla will give up the power?''

''My fear is that he won't. In fact I'm sure he won't. The Contortus family has been in power a long time now; they have acquired too many enemies; they can't afford to give up the power—not to the Senate, not to Balto Fangano, not to anyone. As we've discussed many times before, Drusilla must be using some secret technique in duelling. There is no other way to explain Ignazio's victories. Drusilla won't anticipate defeat. When it comes at last—if we should be so clever or so lucky—he is likely to act on impulse and use whatever force he can to establish a military dictatorship— openly rather than merely under a cloak of constitution- ality as now. And that's where you come in.''

''The island of Gash,'' Robartus said.

Mart nodded—pleased, as always, at the colonel's rapid grasp.

''Four thousand trained Menoma slaves within three hours of the Island of Faltara,'' Mart said. ''By hy- drofoil. Faster by air—but Drusilla may not have the fuel, not if we do our job. In any event, if those men are brought in and unleashed, the Movement will collapse—regardless of the heroism of Cushmen or the population. Men under 'deep command' will let them- selves be slaughtered joyously. Gash must be neu- tralized.''

Robartus raised his eyebrows; his fish-hook scar was red. ''Is that all?'' he asked. ''We can do that just like that.'' He snapped a finger.

Mart wished he could agree. ''There are things about this operation—and Drusilla—that you don't know about. It will take all or most of you to capture and hold the island—under the best of circumstances. That means you will have to take a transport rather than a scout.''

''We planned on that,'' Robartus said. He smiled. ''We anticipated you a little. A transport is a little slower, but it's also easier to 'borrow,' if you see what I mean. And it'll get us there just the same.''

''You will get there, all right,'' Mart said, ''but you may find that you are on a suicide mission. We've discovered recently that Drusilla has a scout. One of our agents lost her life getting us that information—and it's hard intelligence. A scout against a transport is no match. Unless my strategy succeeds, you may never get off the island. And that is why I've hesitated so long in asking you to carry out this mission. The risks are very high.''

Sober faces around the table reflected the gravity of this news. Robartus scratched his scar again, a habit when he was thinking.

''Castle has a scout? Where do they keep it? How on earth did they get it?''

''It's kept in an inner courtyard of the Contortus palace. My guess is that Drusilla got it and knows about it—and not very many other people. I have no idea how they got it, but Drusilla controls a lot of lac. Some general up here on Riondi may have secured a rich retirement, for all I know. Nonetheless, the fact remains. Drusilla has a scout. If he gets suspicious, if he panics, if he decides to use it . . .''

Heads nodded around the table slowly. For a moment there was silence.

''But you have a strategy,'' Robartus said at last.

''Yes,'' Mart said. ''In fact, I have two strategies. One of them depends on you and how you carry out the occupation—and we will come to that. The other one depends on us—and it's a lot more tricky and unpredictable. Any strategy built around the personality of a single man is chancy at best."

"Drusilla?"

"Drusilla. The duel between Balto and Ignazio is designed to accomplish two objectives. The first is to defeat Ignazio, of course—but while that's important, it's not as important as the second one. The deeper strategy is to discredit Drusilla in the eyes of the Contortus family—something that an unsuccessful duel is sure to do, if I read the situation right. We *must* cripple Drusilla—long enough to take over the tundrati. I have designed the whole procedure with that in mind, but I can't be sure. And there are some key unknowns."

"For instance?"

"We might lose the duel, for one. We still don't know the secret of Ignazio's 'longevity'—and we can't afford to wait any longer. For another—Drusilla might stay in power even if Ignazio loses. We don't know how entrenched he is, we don't know how the family members will react. Drusilla has a rival in the household, a certain Solumnos Teck. Teck has been trying very hard to push his boss aside—and we've helped under the table, as it were, by feeding him information now and then. Teck is ambitious, but he might not succeed. And in that case you folks on Gash might be putting your lives on the line."

Robartus screwed up his face. "Is Teck one of us?"

"No. But if he takes over as chief fompus, we have at least an even chance. Teck has been around for years, but I don't think he has a lot of experience. Drusilla hasn't exactly groomed him for leadership."

A young captain spoke up. "If all goes wrong, what do you think will happen? What's the scenario?"

Robartus answered in Mart's stead. "Simple," he said. "Drusilla will overfly the island and give his soldiers the 'deep command.' They will storm us and kill us—sooner or later. Alternatively we might try to get away in the transport, but Drusilla could blast us. Once we're disposed of, Drusilla moves the troops to Faltara. Curtains."

Mart nodded. "That's how I see it too. I am asking you to take a very big chance. I need you there to try to hold the island—but I can't guarantee a thing. With you we have a chance. Without you we may very well fail."

Silence. Robartus had tilted his chair toward the wall and rocked it slowly back and forth. At last he let the chair drop forward and hit the table with a fist. "All right," he cried. "All right, men. What are we all so gloomy about? So we take our chances too—like the rest of the people on Fillippi. And it won't be very different from so called 'routine duty' on Riondi. We may have to tangle with Drusilla and his scout. I am prepared for that. Are you?"

Heads nodded. The officers murmured their assent.

"All right, then. Let's get on with it. Tell us the details, Penta, and don't worry so much about our precious hides. We've got to get you out of here—" he checked his watch "—in twelve minutes or so. Start. We are all ears."

Mart unzipped his jumpsuit. He carried a sheaf of pages under it against his chest. He handed the sheets around the table and began the tactical briefing.

9 — OBEDIENCE IN THE MUSIC ROOM

Obedience, obedience.
—Mistress Sultana

The music room of the Contortus palace lay deep within the women's quarters in West Wing, an oblong room furnished in a style suited to the special fancies of Mistress Sultana. Thick carpets lay on the floor; rugs depicting idyllic scenes (swans, lakes, woods, maidens) hung on the walls; silvery mirrors shimmered between the rugs. Soft hassocks lay all around flanked by mounds of colorful pillows. Against the walls numerous glass tables held lamps, statuettes, and knick-knacks. Instruments cluttered the place lying next to rickety wire-stands that held music scores. The room had no windows. The wall opposite the single door featured elaborately carved panels.

Near the center of the room girls with shaven heads sat in a circle polishing brassware. Mistress Sultana had just departed in a jangle of golden rings and a swoosh of black silk. She had ordered them to work until she returned. She had gone to take her "early evening nap," by which was to be understood an hour or two of peaceful drinking. The girls were most obedient. They worked feverishly, fingers black from polish. White rags flew over jugs, vases, and trays of golden hue. Voices buzzed with mechanical chatter.

Sophie Han sat with the rest, dressed like them in a white silk robe, a red ribbon encircling her body just below her breasts. Her head was also shaven. Unlike the rest she didn't bother polishing the brass. She waited. She imagined Sultana's progress to her room right next to her girls' dormitory. The Mistress would pour herself a glass of wine and sink down on a plush divan opposite a mirror in which she could admire her own skinny form, her own classic profile. She told her girls that she had a classic profile, and they obediently said that yes, she certainly had a classic profile. Sophie gave the mistress time to have three glasses of cicillo. Then she looked up.

"Obedience, obedience," she said, using an imperious tone.

Her words brought immediate silence. The girls assumed rigid postures. Their eyes went vacant, and they fell into a state called "receptivity," an indication that someone had voiced the "deep command" they had been conditioned to obey.

"I will leave now," Sophie said; she spoke in a wooden tone, unable to speak naturally when giving "deep commands." "You won't mention this to anyone. If Sultana returns before I do, you will tell her that I went to the 'little room.' Start working."

The girls woke from the trance-like state and resumed their work and interrupted conversation. They seemed oblivious of Sophie.

Sophie rose and walked to the paneled wall. She placed a thumb on each eye of a carved gargoyle. Under her pressure, the panel moved slowly to the side; an entrance appeared. She slipped through before the secret door was entirely open. On the other side she pushed a button set into the wall, and with a sucking sound the panel closed again.

She hastened along a dark, narrow passageway, sure of every step, her destination a certain stairway cut off by a brick wall some distance from the secret door. Under that stairway she had set up a cramped headquarters for her surreptitious surveillance activities. She had her notebooks hidden there, a flashlight, a few items of street clothing, and a cache of stolen food.

Moving in darkness, she reflected once more on the weird power of the deep command. When they heard the trigger word, Menoma slaves felt a compulsion to obey. Many trigger words were used; they changed from household to household, department to department. Sophie wished she knew all those used by the Contorti; but thus far she could only command the girls of the music room.

She recalled how she had trembled the first time she had used that power, the thrill of success. The girls had acted as if she had been Sultana. Since then she had used the deep command as often as she dared. It gave her some freedom of movement when Sultana took a "nap." The Mistress of the music room was around a good deal; she enjoyed her power. She spent all of her time with the girls; she liked to bask in the innocent adoration she could so easily command. She was the mother hen, the girls her chicks.

Without her secret mission, Sophie would have found this life hard to endure. She too had to fawn on Sultana—but she did it for a reason, not because she had to. She knew herself to be the last in a long line of heroic women sent into this palace as agents. Olaf in the Tower—a tall and cheerful man—had told her of the dangers. She knew about Veronica Dox—whose mutilated body someone had simply pushed into a waste

duct. And she knew what she was looking for—
evidence of some sort of drug that the Contorti used to
make Ignazio invulnerable in duels. But Olaf had urged
her to gather any and all information. "Look for patterns," he had said, "any kind of patterns that seem out
of the ordinary." "Don't expect to run across a little
phial with the label 'duelling elixir,' " he had said,
laughing. "You may have to glean the answer from
tiny little bits and pieces, a word here, a glimpse
there."

Sophie arrived at her secret headquarters. She sat
down on the cold stone beneath the stairway and began
to write hurriedly in the dim glow of the flashlight. She
would soon have to find another; this one was losing
power. Her notebook brimmed with many small observations, none important taken alone. In the aggregate,
they were beginning to add up to the patterns Olaf had
talked about, or at least she thought so.

She knew, for instance, that the household was under
some sort of strain. Some event loomed ahead which
caused anxiety to the chief fompus, Farnit Drusilla. She
couldn't be sure, but she thought that the tension had to
do with the Faltara Games. There would be a duel, and
Ignazio would be one of the contenders. Then at times
she overheard comments hinting that Ignazio would
have no part in it.

As for the fompus, Sophie had become convinced
that he really ruled the household. Ignazio Contortus
was held in great contempt. They called him Blubber,
Grease Ball, and other unflattering names. No one
called Drusilla any names, but the fompus was not
loved. Most of the staff served him loyally—in fear and
trembling. Some few owed allegiance to others. She
overheard such phrases as: "Tinnus? Tinnus is Teck's
man." Or sometimes: "I wouldn't write off Sol, if I

were you. Sol might be chief some day. Maybe soon.'' From such comments she inferred a power struggle between three men: Drusilla, Sol, and Teck. Thus far she had seen neither of the last two.

Other families in Concession, she had discovered, resented the power of the Contorti. Within the household people talked a lot about the Senate. Lord Fantidaimi, leader of the State, wanted to wrest the power from the Controller of Tundrati. Fantidaimi had drafted a constitutional amendment abolishing succession by armed combat. He was too old to fear a challenge, said the fompa, but he couldn't get support for the measure because others were less fearless. Ignazio might challenge. And everyone knew that Ignazio was lucky, lucky beyond measure. This last remark sometimes came accompanied with a snicker, a mocking tone. Those snickers formed one of the pieces Olaf had talked about. So far she couldn't fit it into a pattern.

But the pattern that intrigued her most had to do with East Wing. She had discovered an area down on Third Level surrounded by intense security. She guessed it was a prison complex. People who went Menoma-mad were sent there, never to return. But a prison, taken alone, did not explain the strong taboo that surrounded the place.

She had become alerted to the Third Level mystery soon after her arrival. She had been given special conditioning inside the Contortus palace. She had lain inside a tape machine identical to those she had seen in the Tower. Powerful commands had assaulted her mind, commands to stay away from East Wing. Pictures of the entrance to the forbidden area had been flashed into her mind followed by images of death and horror: skeletons, ghosts, tombstones, snakes, knives dripping blood. A maniacal shrieking laughter had accompanied the visions on the sound track.

Why the special conditioning?

She had heard that a man named Huroka ran the place. She had never seen him, or not knowingly, but she had noted that all the fompa spoke of Huroka with respect. He was a personage to be counted—which only confirmed Sophie's determination to find out more about Huroka's high security domain.

Early in her stay at the palace, she had discovered the extensive network of secret corridors that criss-crossed the warren of buildings forming the Contortus palace. Mistress Sultana used the passages occasionally and openly. When she did not want the girls to notice or to remember something, she merely called "Obedience, obedience," in her reedy voice and commanded her girls to forget that they saw her come or go.

Over a succession of nights, Sophie had explored the entire system of corridors. She dared to leave her bed only when she heard Sultana's high-pitched snore coming from the chamber next to the dormitory. On those excursions she had found several exits to street level, but she hadn't dared to go out. She had nowhere to go, and her shaven head was a give-away. Shaved heads belonged indoors. Castle guards were sure to pick her up. Thus far she hadn't found a suitable hat or scarf to cover her baldness.

Using the corridors, she had approached Third Level East Wing as well—only to discover sealed-off walls. She couldn't enter the forbidden wing from the secret passageways. The entrances could be operated only from the other side.

Sophie finished writing and put her notebook away. Today she had recorded that Drusilla had ordered all superfluous staff to stay behind on Dominus while the family went down to Faltara. But the fompus took all available guards—confirmation that Drusilla anticipated trouble.

She extinguished her flashlight and hurried back to the music room.

Back in the circle of girls Sophie began polishing a heavy brass wine pitcher. It had a single curved handle and a wide pouring spout. In the big round belly of the vessel she could see a comically distorted reflection of herself—the same old face and the new, shaven head. The blazing, yellow mirror surface also reflected parts of the music room and its suffocating, pampered, plush, soft style. Sophie disliked this place. She disliked the ever-present scent of Sultana which hung about the room.

Mistress Sultana had told her girls they need not shave their heads until the household returned from Faltara some weeks from now. They would have a long vacation from the annoying daily scraping chore. The girls had missed one day of shaving, but the novelty of it sufficed to engage them in babbling conversation. They had been talking about hair when Sophie had left; they were still at it.

Sophie worked in silence. The movement of her fingers let her thoughts roam, and as sometimes happened despite her best intentions, her thoughts turned melancholy. She recalled the past—the children she had taught; her parents; beautiful, shining, green Faltara; the panorama of Simalta; the majestic brooding of triple-peaked Crasnus. Underneath her awareness lurked memories of Jan, but she repressed his ghostly presence. She had learned by bitter experience that it was best not to think of him.

Presently the babbling conversation faltered and then died out as everyone fell to listening.

Voices approached—the voice of a male, the reedy tones of Sultana. Unlike her companions, who had little experience of real life save for their sketchy, synthetic memories, Sophie knew that the male was drunk. She felt sudden apprehension; her heartbeat speeded up. Men were excluded from this wing. What could this mean . . .? The voices stopped outside. The door opened, but not all the way. Sultana peered inside. She had been drinking—more than usually. Wine had made red patches on her face and she wore a girlish, silly expression. Someone tickled or pinched her from behind. She turned outward once or twice to shoo her distractor before she finally gave her attention to the girls inside and spoke.

"Obedience, obedience," she fluted; she giggled as someone pinched her again. Her golden rings jangled.

The girls fell into "receptivity." Sophie followed suit, but she observed the door nevertheless as a reflection in her brass pitcher.

"We have some nice visitors tonight," Sultana said, speaking in a sing-song. "You'll entertain these gentlemen and do anything they ask. You'll enjoy it. When the gentlemen leave, you'll forget that they were here. Do it now."

With that Sultana withdrew her head. Whispers sounded beyond the door. Then a heavy-set man dressed in the uniform of a tundratus captain staggered in. Sophie saw a round, fat, purple face. He took up a spread-legged position by the door, his hands on his hips, and surveyed the circle of girls through small glinting eyes.

"Come on in, boys," he cried, glancing to the side.

"Come *on* and just look at all this hot stuff. I've already picked me my sweetie."

His eyes on Sophie, he lurched forward unsteadily. He held out his arms toward her, half stumbled over a ballusa, caught himself, kicked the ballusa aside with a discordant jangle of strings. He came on, a leering, stupid look on his face.

"Come into papa's arms, you luscious, bald bitch," he babbled. "Papa make you haaaappy."

Sophie watched him warily, oblivious of all else.

The captain lurched into the small glass table in front of Sophie's chair. The table fell over and the heavy brass pitcher tumbled off. It rolled toward the door, then stopped as its handle hit the rug. A thick hand grabbed Sophie by the arm and pulled her up roughly. The captain groped for the neck of her white tunic, his aim uncertain. Sophie saw small, blood-shot eyes, the patchy, ruddy face. She saw the tiny hairs of his beard, emerging with evening time. His hand fumbled toward her, his intent to tear the flimsy fabric from her body.

But he didn't get far. Sophie jerked herself loose and attacked him with a fury born of desperation. Her fists flew into the ruddy face. She kicked him in the shin. She darted sideways to escape him.

Her actions were entirely reflexive. She did not—could not—stop to think that by this resistance she revealed herself. No slave under a deep command could behave as she behaved. As she escaped, she realized what she was doing.

The same realization dawned slowly, very slowly on the captain's face. At first his eyes registered incomprehension mixed with pain from her blows and kicks. Then came an expression of surprise. Finally his eyes narrowed and his lips came together.

"So, you little bitch," he croaked. "An agent, are you. Well, I'll take you anyway, and more so."

The circle of slave-girls observed all this with open-mouthed astonishment.

Sophie's kicks and blows had temporarily sobered the drunkard. He lunged at her now with new-found skill and cunning and in a second his arms and body had enveloped her. She struggled without success as they fell onto a hassock. His bristly face bruised hers. His breath, rich with alcohol fumes, threatened to suffocate her. His hands, at her back, tore and ripped her gown.

Then she heard a sound as of a dull gong. Immediately the captain's body went limp, his arms relaxed. His entire weight sagged over her, taking her breath away. But this lasted only a second. Someone rolled the body to the side. It fell to the floor with a dull thud. Sophie looked up at her rescuer, still in a helpless position on the hassock.

He stood immediately before her, a lithe young man in a red tundratus jacket. On his collar he wore the platypus emblem. In his hand he held a heavy brass pitcher.

He was Jan Rigg.

What the rapacious attack of the captain had not accomplished, the sight of Jan almost did. Sophie nearly fainted. His face too reflected shock and unbelief. Then she saw his eyes explode in joy. He sees that I've escaped Menoma, she thought. He thinks that it's a miracle. .

Sophie was right. Jan could not believe his eyes—his luck. There she lay before him, as beautiful as ever, her shapely limbs a bit awry, her body wrapped in silky folds, her arms so full. She had lost her hair somehow but she was Sophie and she knew him. She still knew him. Touched by unbearable emotion, he lifted her from the orange hassock and took her into his arms.

Dull groaning sounds issuing from Captain Brudd aroused Jan from temporary bliss. He sensed the danger they were in, an urgency to act. Sophie had the same emotion.

"You must escape, " she whispered. "Quickly. I'll show you the way."

"I can't," he said. "I have to take him back with me." Jan gestured toward the figure on the floor. He felt sick suddenly. Hitting the captain was inexcusable. He had violated his orders. To leave the Captain lying here would compound the error.

The captain stirred. Jan hesitated, his mind racing, his face tense. Then he picked up the brass pitcher and hit the captain again. The brass gave forth a mournful bong. Jan shivered. The captain sagged back to the floor like a sack. Blood discolored the back of his head.

"Fillip," Jan called, shaking off his disgust. "Help me. Get him up—on my back."

Sophie watched. She hadn't even noticed the second young man until now, an earnest-looking chubby fellow. Her emotions were in turmoil—she lacked the famous Tessori control just now.

"Hurry up." she called, half-whispering. Then she led the way to the secret door.

Moments later they were in the darkness of the passage. Sophie went ahead; Jan huffed behind her under the heavy body across his shoulder; Fillip brought up the rear.

Hastily, pressed by the danger that surrounded them like the stone of these dark halls, Sophie told her story in quick, breathless sentences. She told Jan about Phila, her assignment, and her notebooks full of intelligence.

Jan stopped. He lowered the unconscious captain and laid him on the cold stone floor.

"You're part of Cush?" he asked.

"Yes," she said. She could barely see him.

"Me too," he said. Then he told his story, not caring just now whether Fillip heard or not.

"Look, Sophie," he said at the end. "You come with us. You will be safe with the Fanganos."

Sophie shook her head. "I can't," she said. "Not without a scarf or wig—and not if you are carrying a body. Come back tonight—well past midnight—and bring me some clothing and something for my head. But now—please let's hurry."

Fillip moved forward. He took Brudd's legs while Jan lifted the captain by slack arms. Brudd had been badly damaged and didn't even groan.

"What about Paulus?" Fillip asked.

"Paulus has to fend for himself," Jan said. "We can't worry about him just now." They had left Paulus with that awful woman, that Sultana. Paulus would have his hands full.

Sophie had moved ahead. She found the small door leading to the street. She felt the stone wall carefully until her hand chanced on the button that would activate the lock. She trembled with impatience listening to the huffing and puffing of the two men as they approached.

"Here," she whispered. "In here." Then she pushed the button.

Jan groped toward her and embraced her quickly. "Tonight," he said. "well past midnight."

She nodded. "Be out here," she said. "Tap on the wall."

"I'll be here. But Sophie—just in case something happens, remember: the Fangano household. They are in the southwest district and their emblem is the platypus. Remember that. Ask for Leo, the chief fompus. Just in case."

She nodded quickly. "*Please*." she whispered. "Go now." She pointed out into a dark alley the sliding door had revealed.

It was after the panel had closed again with a sucking sound and Sophie had turned back that she realized her omission. She had left the music room without commanding the girls to obedience.

God, what a fool I am, she thought angrily.

She broke into a run down the corridor, praying, praying that she would arrive in time.

She bruised her arms on the stone walls in the darkness. At times she nearly tripped and fell. She arrived at the music room wall gasping and sweating. She pressed the button and stepped through the moment she could.

The circle of girls was still intact. They were busy polishing brass. But in their midst now sat Mistress Sultana.

10 — POTSLA RUN'S FINEST

Poor Glitsch. Poor dear Glitsch. You'll never be a jouster, that's for sure.

—Jan Rigg

He sat in the bleachers dressed in the fompus robes, his identity hidden beneath a wig and a red beard glued to his cheeks and upper lips by an ill-smelling elastomer. The sun was up, the turf below a brilliant green. Voices murmured all around. The scents were lovely. Nonetheless Jan had dropped into a brood.

He roused himself.

Be a man, he told himself, be a man of Cush. Remember the mission. Trust the people, trust your luck. She will be all right. I'm sure she will be all right.

Three days had passed since that awful night below the wall of the Contortus palace when he had waited in the alley holding a sack of clothing—and she hadn't come. He had waited until early light, until he couldn't wait any longer without running intolerable risks. Then, sadly, he had left again.

Ever since then he had told himself at intervals that she would be all right. Something had prevented her escape that night, but there would be other nights. Fompus Leo had insisted that Jan go down to Potsla Run, but he had promised to leave behind guards who had Sophie's description. They would hold lookout "for the lady," as Leo had put it, and radio the family the moment she showed up.

"Yesterday you thought she was a slave without her memories," Leo had said. "Today you know that she escaped that fate. You are a lucky man. Trust your luck—and don't let anything divert you from the mission."

So Jan had flown down to Faltara using the Fangano chopper. From there the Run's levi-limo had whisked him to the ranch. And here he was—amidst familiar scenes and smells—feeling a momentary panic once again.

The mission comes first, the mission comes first, the mission comes first. He spoke the words inwardly, a litany of self-assurance. After a while the clump of darkness deep within him disappeared. He could concentrate on the action before him.

The annual auction at Potsla Run was always a festive event. Felina and lox hunts occupied the lords and ladies during the initial day; that night they feasted at a noisy banquet and usually danced till dawn. The second day belonged to the racers. They ran in demonstration all day long and were sold that evening. Jan had waited to see Glitsch among the racers. When Glitsch had failed to show, he guessed that the beast would be held off the market this year. Perhaps he needed training as a racer. Or some fool planned to fix that shying—a hopeless task. Jan had worked his heart out and had failed.

The third day, by tradition, was reserved for the jousters. Jousters were the cream of the crop, and this year's crop the finest ever.

Seated next to Balto, Jan had watched jousters circling and hitting since eleven in the morning. Their hoofs had torn up the turn in magnificent displays of volta. The first dozen had been good animals—the least of them superior to Snoorok, the Fangano's best animal. At noon came a break. Attendants in yellow tunics piped in silver served lunch. Jan knew them all by name—despite their powdered wigs. Then boys dressed in spiffy silver-and-blue uniforms blew alarms to announce the second round. Now came the real jousters—the cream of the crop.

The crowd stirred. Sondus Rigg and Jaimo Potsla presented leather-bound folders to important guests, Balto among them. Jan stole a glance at his stocky father and thought he saw a trace of sadness, a shadow of grief below the headman's now professionally friendly expression.

Balto leafed through various folders while Jan surveyed the crowd. Concession families filled the stands. In their bright robes—silver and gold and white and blue—they made a bright assembly. Parasols of many colors hung above them. Tundrati in bright red tunics formed up on either side of the stands ensured their security. The crowd buzzed; people looked toward a wooden wall at one end of the field.

In his tafchuko days Jan had waited behind that wall many a time. He recalled how the crowd had sounded from that vantage point, recalled his nervous impatience as he had waited for the signal to move. Now he was a fompus in the stands sipping tea through straws. Hard to believe . . .

Behind a crackling force field to Jan's right sat the Contortus contingent. Only the Contorti needed such protection; everyone else braved the beam of an assassin without electromagnetic shielding. Streak-haired

Ignazio slouched in the center; his eyes wandered. Next to him sat Farnit Drusilla. Jan had learned to recognize the man by a burnished skull and a stilted gait.

Balto had told him to watch especially a small, wrinkled, rat-like man next to Drusilla, his lips ever a-whisper at Drusilla's ear.

"That's Huroka," Balto had explained. "We don't know what his function is, but he's a sinister little rodent. When Ignazio duels he's always around. The rest of the time he stays in his hole."

Jan studied Huroka's screwed-up, crabby, angry face. He wondered if the men understood anything about the beasts.

"Here, take a look at this," Balto now rumbled. "That's the one for us. It says here that you trained him."

Jan took the foler and almost started. The gold letters on the blue tafpa leather said GLITSCH. He couldn't believe that the Run would offer Glitsch for sale as a jouster. There must be some mistake, some error. He opened the folder.

Sure enough, it was Glitsch, *his* Glitsch. Sired by Frotsch who was sired by Tluk who was sired by the legendary Snart . . . bearing on his forehead a mark renowned in Fillippi's jousting history . . . can be said without exaggeration to be one of the best, possibly *the* best jouster . . . his unparalleled speed, his unsurpassed "pace-shift" mark Glitsch as . . .

Jan's eyes ran down the page. Here it was: trained by Januario Sondus Phanto Rigg, ridden today by Silesius Veronicus Halmo Rigg.

He glanced in the lower left-hand corner: Suggested starting bid, C 15,000.

Fifteen thousand credits! Ye Gods!

Jan felt dismay. How could Sondus offer Glitsch? And with such puffed advertisement. At such a price!

If Glitsch held true before the lance, he might deserve the billing and the money. But Glitsch shied. Every time. Jan was convinced of that.

He turned to Balto even as the trumpets started again and a glorious blue beast shot out from behind the wooden wall, urged forward by his rider with the traditional "Hay, Hay, Hay."

"Glitsch may or may not be the beast for us," Jan said. "My bet is on Fleatcher. Look at his folder. I'll point him out to you later. There's something about Glitsch I'll have to explain to you, but first I want to see something."

The rider in the field went around the circle in a warm-up exercise. He held his lance in the vertical, its butt resting on his saddle. He bobbed and rocked unevenly in random rhythm with the unpredictable tafpa trot. Jan recognized the beast. It was Porusht.

Meanwhile attendants mounted a man-shaped figure on a single dummy at the right of the field. They put the mannikin where normally the straw bale would be. They arranged it so that it appeared to hold the dummy's lance.

Then the rider hit his beast, and the tafpa came alive. Its three humps began to secrete the panic hormone, and the hormone spread throughout its body carried by the blood. The rider let out the volta cry: "Hee, hee, hee, hee," he cried in fast stacatto. He lowered his lance and leaned forward. The ungainly beast had lost its graceless movements. It churned around the track at ever growing speed, its six legs nearly invisible, a blurr of sinew and muscle. Rider and mount went around twice more at increasing speed. Then the tafpa turned left in a swift pace-change—a leap into the air and a twisting turn—and the pair came hurtling toward the dummy.

A beautiful charge! The animal never hesitated, didn't slow. The dummy's lance flew aside. The rider's weapon pierced the mannikin and lifted it clear off the dummy in a shower of sawdust. The beast shot past the dummy without losing a step.

Jan smiled in admiration. That's how it was done. It had been a while since he had seen such a fine tafpa and such an exhibition of tafchuko skill. That would be Rinotto, a topnotch trainer. The collision had been faultless.

Then, in succession, came a dozen excellent animals. From time to time Jan leaned over to Balto and gave him some comment or other. Wigged attendants brought more lac tea, crisp baguse bacon, and sour Shaman strips. Jan kept note of Huroka's doings, tried to see when the ratty fellow spoke to the bald fompus. Pudgy Ignazio appeared to be asleep.

Fleatcher came and confirmed Jan's earlier judg-ment. Truly a fine beast. But the crowd failed to ap-preciate Jan's favorite. Fleatcher had a smallish, heavy look and lacked the aristocratic bearing of most jous-ters. And in the brief exhibition Fleatcher's virtues didn't show. Jan knew them nonetheless—steadiness, strength (important in carrying a big man like Balto), an even temper, an aggressive spirit, and responsive-ness.

Huroka took no interest in Fleatcher. Was that dis-sembling or true indifference? Jan couldn't tell. The Fanganos knew very little about the fellow. Was he a tafchuko? He certainly had the small, wiry build for it.

Any true tafchuko would see that Fleatcher was a winner.

And then came Glitsch.

Jan watched his old buddy with concentration but gave no outward sign of interest. Just possibly Sil had cured that shying. Miracles were possible. After all he had found Sophie again—and she was still herself.

When Glitsch broke into the volta the crowd responded with a roar. Sil made five rounds around the oval, a special distinction. Parts of the crowd stood up and clapped—a natural reaction. Glitsch was spectacular—such grace, such speed! Glitsch stood out by a visible margin!

Then Sil took Glitsch into the left turn and up against the mannikin. Immediately following collision, as the spectators rose to their feet and broke into spontaneous, enthusiastic applause, Jan pointed toward Glitsch excitedly and leaned toward Balto.

"I want you to nod at what I say, Balto," he whispered. "Act pleased."

Balto obliged. He nodded vigorously. He smiled broadly. He said: "Why all this? I presume it's for Contortus consumption?"

"Yes."

"Is something wrong with Glitsch? I'm no expert, of course, but that beast is beautiful. The finest I've seen yet."

"I'll explain it to you later," Jan said. "When we are alone."

He had seen Glitsch shy. At that speed and from this distance only a very experienced eye could have picked up the flaw. Jan had worked Glitsch so many hours he knew the beast's every move. And he had seen that characteristic tilt to the right, a tilt that would become pronounced by the third round of a joust. In the fifth and final round, with Glitsch tiring, it would be clearly visible to anyone.

Jan wondered if Huroka had seen it. If he was a real tafchuko, he couldn't have missed it.

11 — QUADRUS IN QUANDARY

Priority Five, Infiltration: It is our goal to place sympathizers or actual agents at middle to high administrative levels of all major activities controlled or influenced by Concession. This means, above all, and in this order (1) the fompas, (2) officers of the armed forces, (3) managers of lac plantations, (4) spaceport and airport managers, and (5) owners of domestic industrial plants. Extreme caution in recruiting and reliance on ideological persuasion must be used to obtain the cooperation of this privileged layer of Fillippi society.

—Third Annual Strategy Study of Cush

From the forty-first floor of the Faltara Tower, Potsla Run appeared in the distance like a giant T bounded by forests and criss-crossed by fencing. Clusters of buildings formed clusters of light under old trees. The oval training fields and long barns lay in gathering shadow. The moving lights and rising smoke marked the auction field.

Two junior fompa standing at the window of the Tower gazed in the direction of Potsla Run but did not look at it. They contemplated the larger view—the shimmering ocean in the distance, the blood red reflection of the setting sun. The sky had darkened. Dominus hovered in that darkness, alive with a sprinkling of lights.

The fompa conversed in low tones. Despite their meditative pose at the window, they appeared tense.

"The next three weeks will be the roughest," said Olaf, the taller of the two.

Sallust, the shorter, nodded. "I can take the danger," he said. "It's the waiting I can't stand. I keep waiting for Drusilla to call me up to Castle. I have nightmares about that guy."

"He is down there," Olaf said; he pointed toward Potsla Run. "Thank God for the joust. It keeps Drusilla busy. So long as the old boy worries about the challenge, he won't bother us."

Sallust seemed to shiver. "Busy or not, I'm scared. Too damn many people are involved. It's not like the old days, Olaf. You know . . . smuggling a man or woman through the Conditioning every now and then. Now we're dealing with these masses. Anything can go wrong. The whole thing could go sky high."

Olaf chuckled. His companion had no idea just how great the risks had grown. The same phenomenon was taking place on seven islands, in seven towers. He turned his back on the sunset.

"Think of it as a great historic moment," he said. "And here you are, little Sallust Manpost, doing your part in the midst of it. You will be a hero when all of this is over. Dream about that. Dream about the parade."

Sallust looked more concerned than dreamy. "Can Richter keep the lid on?"

"Don't worry about Richter. He is an old hand at revolution. Come on," Olaf said, changing his tone. "Let's get out of here and grab a bite. Then we'd better sneak down to the Conditioning Rooms. Our boys need tender loving care. Did you ever imagine that we'd be training Cushmen in the *Tower?*"

Sallust sighed. "No," he said. "That's what scares me."

"Oh, Sallust," Olaf said, shaking his head. "You're a worry wart. Don't worry. The end is in sight."

They made for the door past two desks placed back to back. The door flew open just before they reached it. Another young fompus burst in. He had very short blond hair and a peachy, boyish complexion ravaged now by blotches of emotion.

"I've had it," he cried, striding with purpose toward a desk. He threw himself into a chair; "I'm through."

Olaf eyed the newcomer with a questioning expression.

"Just back from seeing Richter," the peach-faced fompus volunteered. "I guess I should have asked for your permission, Olaf, but I didn't. When it comes to bucking the chain of command, you're as gutless as a hindi leclair."

Olaf smiled and leaned back against a file cabinet. "You can see Richter any time you want to, Quadrus. You don't need my permission. What's the matter? Why the uproar?"

Quadrus looked at Olaf with hatred in his eyes. "You know perfectly well what it is—and I've told you countless times. And don't you tell me I'm overworked. I don't buy that any more. I have eyes," he cried, pointing a finger at each of his eyes. "I put things together. Something stinks around here. Something stinks."

Olaf raised his eyebrows. "*That* again? Your subjective reaction to the last batch of tundrati? You're being a little paranoid, you know."

Quadrus was genuinely irritated. "Look here, Olaf," he cried, slapping the desk with the flat of his hand; the blotches on his face turned a darker red. "'Subjective reaction'—hell! It's that plus a lot of other things. I'm sick and tired of repeating this, but here goes again." He held a finger in the air. "One," he said, "all the officers have been replaced in the last three weeks; *all* of them, Olaf. Two, all the fompa in this tower are new. You two are the only ones from the old days. Three. Slaves work their way out of the kinesthetic machines. From everything I know, that's supposed to be impossible. Four. The Menoma storage room was flooded! Why? I could go on and on."

"Well, don't," Olaf said. He gave a sigh of boredom. "I've heard it all before. You say you went to see Richter. Very well. What did he say?"

Quadrus snorted. "He is as gutless as a hindi leclair. He told me to forget it. He said it was just coincidence. Well, sir, I am *not* going to forget it. I am going to the top with this. I know my orders. We have to report unusual observations. All the way to the top, if necessary."

Sallust interjected himself into the conversation. His voice quavered slightly. "What do you propose to do?"

"I'm going to call Drusilla, that's what I'll do. I'll tell him flat out that our tundrati don't act like Menoma slaves. They work themselves out of machines, they rip conditioning wires off their heads, they laugh and joke during the first formation. And I'll tell him that we've had a change of staff and that Richter is as gutless as, as gutless as—"

"A hindi leclair," Olaf said. Then he looked at Sallust, trying to catch the man's eyes. Quadrus would not be calmed this time; action would have to be taken. Sallust seemed frozen.

Olaf looked at Quadrus. "If I were you, Quadrus, I would sleep on it," he said. "You're in a state and Drusilla is up to his ears in the Potsla Run auction. He won't appreciate a junior official calling him about his intuitions—by-passing six layers of command."

Quadrus took this as a challenge. He glared. "You want to bet? I'll bet you he will listen. Watch me. Listen to what he'll say."

He leaned forward and pulled a visiphone toward himself. He punched numbers rapidly. A stupid Menoma-face appeared. "Directory," the woman said.

"Potsla Run," Quadrus demanded. "Emergency."

"I'll connect you," she said.

Olaf looked at Sallust again and raised his eyebrows. "This has gone far enough. Don't you think so, Sallust?" The tone was calm and conversational; too calm, too conversational. Quadrus looked up suspiciously.

Olaf smiled mysteriously, hoping to unbalance Quadrus. Another one, he thought. The Tower's dungeons already crawled with scores of the old guard. Their care and feeding took more and more time. Another one would have to join their ranks.

The screen came alive in color and resolved itself into the image of a very young stable boy. "P-p-potsla R-r-run," he stuttered.

"Yes, Sallust," Olaf said, in the same easy-going tone, "Quadrus has just made a big mistake. Wouldn't you agree?"

Sallust didn't answer; he stood by the door, eyes on the floor. Sallust was a fine technician but a poor man of action.

From the stable boy's perspective, the screen showed part of the shoulder and a portion of the profile of peach-faced Quadrus. The boy didn't know what to say.

"I hope you will agree with me," Olaf said. He set himself in motion toward the second desk; he moved slowly, carefully, like an animal trainer. "I do hope you'll agree with me, Sallust. Quadrus needs to be disciplined. A little house-arrest is what this calls for."

"S-s-sir," the stable boy stammered.

Olaf opened a desk drawer and reached into it. He kept his eyes on Quadrus and hoped that Sallust would stop the young fompus if he got wise and tried to flee.

Quadrus also sensed that something was wrong. "What's this all about," he cried. The color had drained from his face.

He didn't get an answer. Olaf's hand came out of the drawer. It held a strange device, shaped like a gun. It hissed sharply as Olaf pulled the trigger. A tiny drug-dart penetrated Quadrus' neck. Quadrus slapped himself as if stung by an insect. In that attitude his eyes suddenly glazed over and then closed. He sank slowly to the surface of the desk; his face gradually assumed an angellic expression.

Olaf moved to the visiphone. "Is this the Mollono Ranch?"

The stable boy shook his head vigorously. "Potsla Run," he said.

"Sorry, wrong number." Olaf clicked off the machine. He looked over at Sallust and raised his shoulders in a shrug. "Like I said—the next three weeks will be the roughest."

12 — THE AUCTION

Low bid, high bid, what'm I bid? Do I hear fifteen, sixteen, seventeen, eight?

—*Potsla Run auctioneer*

As darkness fell, Balto and Jan joined the crowd of lords and fompa gathered on the sloping lawn above the auction ring. Jan wore his uniform again—the red-haired wig, the beard, and the blue robe of a junior fompus. He studied the auction list stable boys were hawking for nine credits a piece. Glitsch stood in the middle of the list—far enough down to hold the crowd, soon enough in the sequence to inspire spirited bidding. Fleatcher came toward the end. The crowd's reaction to this afternoon performance had earned him a tail-end spot.

The scene was festive.

Ryant bulls turned roasting over three large pits filled with aromatic ropewood in white heat; the burnt-orange meat dripped fat into the fire, and the mouth-watering smell drifted across the lawn. Tables stood ready with colorful table-cloths that reached down to the ground; padded benches had been set up around them. Attendants carried spouted buckets of flavored cicillo to encourage heavy drinking. A band played on dulicet, viola, harp, and trumpet on a raised platform.

Sondus and Jaimo Potsla circulated among the guests, each dressed in traditional tafchuko garb—ruffled shirt, blue britches, boots, tafchuko hat. As elder statesmen of the tafchuko community, each also wore a wide red ribbon draped from shoulder to waist. Emblems hung on the ribbons—mementoes of prizes and races won in Potsla Run's distinguished history. Other trainers also mingled, talking. Potsla Run was warming up the customers—drink, food, music, and "every tafchuko a salesman."

Soon attendants ran from the pits to the tables. They carried roast ryant on silver trays—smokey, steaming platters. The crowd ate. Then as darkness closed in altogether, servants appeared carrying lampoons raised high on poles. The guests began to drift slowly toward the auction ring at the bottom of the slope, beyond the glowing pits.

The auction was held around a circle covered with sawdust. Three-quarters of the area was occupied by seats facing the cut-off trunk of a giant ponok tree. Once the auction began, the auctioneer stood on the stump flanked by servants holding lights. From this vantage point he could oversee the audience over the humps of the animal under consideration. The tafpa always stood in the center of the circle held by a stable boy.

Now the auctioneer, a tall, gangly fellow, stood next to the tall ponok stump, his arm resting on its surface. He held conversation with stout, stocky Sondus. Guests were filling the seats, and servants positioned themselves with lampoons among them to provide illumination. But for good measure, two giant bonfires had been lit on left and right, some distance from the scene. Their flickering flames created a dance of large shadows in the circle.

Balto and Jan found seats and searched the place for the Contorti. They found Drusilla and Huroka to the right, flanked by lesser officials. Neither Ignazio nor other members of the family were present; Blubber Boy was too precious to risk in so open an assembly, Balto said. "And," he added with a chuckle, "it's embarrassing to sit under a force-umbrella on such an occasion." Jan answered that the Contorti were safe enough. After all, they had a ring of palace guards between themselves and lesser mortals; the guards were armed with beamers. Then he asked if Balto could identify the senior fompus with the slicked-down black hair who was seated next to Huroka.

"That, my friend, is Solumnos Teck, the one I was telling you about this afternoon," Balto said. "I bet Drusilla isn't pleased to have him here. Teck looks out for the other members of the family."

Jan nodded. Balto had worked out a strategy that afternoon designed to make Drusilla look foolish. Balto would bid for Glitsch to the limit of the Fangano cash reserves, forcing Drusilla to pay dearly for a flawed beast. Teck would use that fact as ammunition in the family's internal political battle—sooner or later. Jan was happy to have learned something about his mission during these last few days.

A steady stream of lords stopped by the Contortus contingent to shake hands and to visit. None came by to greet Balto Fangano, but all the lords looked at him from time to time. For this occasion Balto had consented to break with his usual rustic tradition. Instead of grey overalls he wore a black jumpsuit—black because this was a somewhat formal occasion. He stood out among the robed assembly. To be seen in his company was to invite Drusilla's wrath. ''They don't dare talk to me,'' Balto told Jan, ''but eight out of ten Castle-lords wish me well in the joust, I can assure you of that.''

The auction began with a trumpet blast. Jaimo Potsla was helped up on the stump by stable-boys and gave a little speech. He welcomed his guests to this, the hundred and third, Potsla Run jouster auction. He recalled some of the great animals that had been sold here and he named their illustrious owners. Then he talked about the animals on the list this year. He spoke of Glitsch in glowing terms and heads turned to look at Balto once again. Then Jaimo bid everyone good hunting and jumped off the ponok stump with an old man's groan. The auctioneer clambered up to take his place. As the first animal was led in, he began his high-pitched song:

''Low bid, high bid, what'm I bid? Do I hear four, four, four-five, five . . .''

At first the pace was halting. Buyers learned the pitch-man's rhythm. He, in turn, took the crowd's measure, spotted the buyers, and learned to recognize individual signals. Then as the first and second tafpa were sold, the pace picked up.

Jan had attended many auctions and thought that he could gauge the mood of such assemblies. Perhaps he was very tense, perhaps it was really so—but he felt that the excitement of this auction was greater than he had ever experienced; and the tension mounted as tafpa after tafpa was disposed of and the name of Glitsch came nearer and nearer.

According to the strategy they had worked out that afternoon, Balto bought one tafpa early. It was Poruscht. They had chosen Poruscht because he came early in the bidding and would make Drusilla wonder what they were planning to do. They also needed two good tafpas—one for Balto, one for Jan; one for the joust, one in reserve. Poruscht cost them six thousand credits, which left them a cash reserve of forty-thousand credits—enough by far to buy *both* Glitsch and Fleatcher if it came to that, Jan thought.

The Contorti didn't contest the sale of Poruscht, but they followed the transaction with evident interest. Through gaps in the guarding tundrati around the contingent, Jan saw Drusilla turn his head. The lights reflected in his burnished skull, the shadows played over his face, a face of carnivorous intensity reminiscent of a high-flying goyla. Then Drusilla turned to rat-like Huroka with a curt remark.

The auction went on, and now the auctioneer was selling Niyast. After Niyast came Glitsch. Niyast should have brought six to seven thousand credits, but the bidding failed to catch fire and died at four thousand five hundred. Everyone waited for Glitsch. The auctioneer tried hard to raise the price. He worked for a commission calculated as a percent above the minimum price—the price in the folders. He found no takers and dispatched the tafpa with a triple "sold."

Jan searched the darkness to the right—the spot Glitsch would come from. All heads were turned in that direction. The murmuring stopped abruptly when a stable-boy in a silver-and-blue uniform led Glitsch into the auction ring. Glitsch came on his six legs, his three humps overlaid with ribbons all around; his blue fur, now almost black in the flickering darkness, shone from vigorous grooming. As the boy stopped in the middle of the ring, Glitsch turned his head toward the crowd. It seemed to Jan that the huge red eyes were trying to find him and that the sixteen small nostrils of the beast sucked in Jan's familiar smell. The crowd seemed to be holding its breath.

"Low bid, high bid, what'm I bid? Do I hear fifteen for this splendid beast, yes, sixteen, gents, seventeen, yes, seventeen folks, do I hear eighteen, yessir, eighteen, yes, high bid, yes, nineteen, low bid, yes, gents, low, gents, nineteen, do I hear twenty, twenty it is, twenty—"

"Thirty thousand credits."

The deep rumbling voice belonged to Balto. The assembly gasped; the auctioneer stopped babbling. Silence. Thirty thousand credits—a near record for a jouster! Jan remembered the sale of Schlumad many years ago. Schlumad had brought thirty-four. Now no one dared to bid.

"Thirty thousand, high bid, low—" the auctioneer began, unsure of himself. Whatever loss he had sustained with Niyast he had made up in a hurry. He felt himself losing control of the situation. "Thirty, high, do I hear thirty-one, thirty-one—"

Then the crowd heard a rasping voice call, "Thirty one." The bidder was Huroka.

"Thirty two."

"Three."

"Thirty-four."

"Thirty-nine," rasped Huroka.

It all went so fast that the crowd could barely give expression to its astonishment, its thrill. Balto did not respond immediately, and in the silence the vast sum of money floated invisibly over Glitsch in the center. Glitsch seemed unaware of the excitement he caused. He kicked peacefully with his central pair of legs.

"Enough" Jan whispered to Balto through his teeth, through his false beard. But Balto waved him to silence with a big hand. Unnatural excitement covered the big man's ordinarily placid face. Jan wished that Balto would be sensible. They were within a thousand credits of their limit. If Drusilla dropped out of the bidding, they would be left with flawed Glitsch and Poruscht. But Balto wouldn't be stopped.

"Forty," he rumbled.

"Fifty."

"Sixty-five." (The man has gone mad, Jan thought. He has lost his mind.)

"Seventy."

"and Five."

"Eighty."

The rapid sequence of calls came to a halt abruptly as the Contorti hesitated. Jan had seen Solumnos Teck reach out a hand to stop Huroka from going on. Now Teck leaned forward and argued with Drusilla. His hand shook as he gestured, light sparkled in his pasted-down black hair and rimless glasses.

Jan's guts grew tight. He stopped breathing. What if they stopped now? What if they didn't go on? What would Penta say if Balto bought Glitsch at a price never yet paid for a tafpa on Fillippi. Balto's face was a study in odd excitement. His eyes glinted; his placid features were stiff with tension.

Then Huroka raised his head.

"One hundred thousand credits for Glitsch," he rasped.

Jan grabbed Balto's arm in a steely grip, oblivious of the groan that surged over the crowd. "Let them have it, for God's sake," he urged, breathless with anxiety. The sweat flowed freely under his wig and false beard.

Balto turned to Jan. He seemed entranced. Once more Jan whispered: "Stop, for God's sake." Balto then seemed to awaken.

"I think I agree with you, Jan," he rumbled in a normal, conversational tone. "We've probably stretched our luck far enough. But let's just confer together a little longer. It'll put pressure on Drusilla. What, by the way, is the highest price every paid for a tafpa?"

"You don't *know* that? For God's sake, lord, this bid is three times the record."

Balto chuckled. "You don't say! We *are* lucky. Luck must have deserted the Contorti for once."

As they whispered, the pressure built and built. All eyes were turned in their direction. The auctioneer stood on his stump, a long, skinny figure, bypassed by the world. Then a voice called sharply:

"You heard the bid, auctioneer, what are you waiting for. Do your job."

Jan didn't recognize the voice. "Drusilla," Balto whispered.

As if stung, the dazed auctioneer came alive.

"Oh," he cried, expressing the emotion of the crowd, an emotion of shameless astonishment. "Oh, ladies and lords, the high bid is one-oh-oh, do I hear one-oh-one, one, one. High bid, low bid, what'm I bid, one-oh-one? one-oh-one."

"Get on with it, man, don't stall." This was Drusilla once again.

"Yes, lord, oh, yes, lord. Glitsch is selling at one hundred thousand credits. Selling . . . selling . . . SOLD!"

The crowd broke into applause, compelled to release tension in some tangible way. Amidst the clapping, the Contortus contingent now rose as a body and, led by Drusilla, made for the guest compound behind the crowd on top of the slope. Several Castle-lords broke away from the assembly and ran after Drusilla to shake his hand. The fompus stopped to accept congratulations, but he did so without visible emotion, with curt nods. He didn't appear to be overjoyed.

The rest of the auction went quickly and without spirit. The guests drifted away. Balto acquired Fleatcher for twelve thousand credits. Then he and Jan also left. As they walked up the sloping lawn, out of the hearing of others, Balto broke into loud laughter, laughter so hard it doubled him over.

13 — THIRD LEVEL EAST WING

Third Level East Wing No No Ghosts Death Ghouls Blood Stay Clear Deepest Command Shreeeeek.
            —Voice on Contortus conditioning tape.

Deep in the bowels of the Contortus palace, Sophie stirred in her cell. As sleep faded, her body grew restless. She turned on the cool floor this way and that; her hands groped for a blanket in half-sleep to cover her nakedness, but she had neither blanket or bed, only the rubbery floor. Her movements slowly brought her awake. She opened her eyes in the total darkness; panic seized her for a terrible moment, and she rolled herself into a little ball. She had no idea where she was or who she was.

Then, without much sensory support except the feel of the cool floor and an awareness of her own body— which she hugged with both arms in her fading terror—she remembered everything. She was on Third Level, East Wing, and this darkness was her home. She had been in this cell—oh, several days. Hunger had awakened her, and soon she would be fed . . .

Slowly she relaxed her body. She rose to her knees and crawled to the wall where she sat down with her back against its pliable surface. Breathing exercises tended to calm her, and now she gained a semblance of inner control of breathing. Next she turned to a contemplation of her mission. In her deprived state—without light, without objects to touch, and with virtually no sound in her cell—she depended for her sanity on a continuous preoccupation with the immediate past and the immediate future.

"I am here because I made a mistake," she said aloud. The soft walls swallowed her voice. "But," she assured herself, "the Master says that mistakes are the womb of opportunity."

And it was true. She had achieved one of her goals—even if not in the manner she had planned; she had penetrated Third Level, East Wing. Unfortunately she had no freedom to explore it.

She examined the past, seeking for patterns again. Once more she raced down the secret corridor toward the music room, once more she bruised her arms on the rough stone, once more she sweated from exertion and anxiety. Then she stood at the hinged panel and pressed the button—and there was another mistake. She had failed to peer through the spy-hole first and thus failed to note Sultana's return, and that was the beginning of her predicament. She had blundered through that door; in that moment Sultana's obedient little pups rose to attack, and then she had stood there like a fool, held by sixteen pairs of tightly clutching hands around her arms, legs, and ankles. Then came Sultana looking like a maddened fury, a jangle of rings, a swish of black silk, an odor of cicillo mingled with the smell of fear.

"You bitch," Sultana spat from the pit of her stomach; her skinny hand drew back; a sharp ring cut Sophie's cheek and drew a tiny line of blood. "You *dare* endanger me! Lucky for me the household isn't here. Drusilla will never hear about *you!* Right, girls?"

Hands tightened around Sophie's limbs; shaved heads bobbed in abject obedience.

"How did you get in here? Who sent you? Why did you pick *my* group?" Sultana's crazed dark eyes stared at Sophie with fear and hatred. "You. will. tell. me!" Sultana cried, and her hand rose for another savage slap. Sophie closed her eyes before the bony hand tore into her face again.

Stung by pain, Sophie concentrated. The girls would kill and then dismember her—probably in the shower room. I will end up in the waste, she thought, like Veronica Dox!

"So you won't talk, my bird," Sultana hissed. "We will see how long you can hold out." Sultana took a long, sharp needle from the bun of hair atop her oblong skull. Holding the needle by the coral ball in which it ended, she approached with the obvious intention of destroying Sophie's eyes.

Sophie braced herself. "Obedience, obedience," she cried. "Let me go, you zombies. Kill *her*—kill Sultana."

The order worked just long enough to permit Sophie's escape. Sultana retreated a step, surprised, and Sophie lunged forward as sweaty hands released her. She burst through the door, heard Sultana scream, then heard the choking, reedy voice call for obedience in turn. By the time the slave girls resumed their chase, Sophie had gained a tiny edge.

She saw herself in memory running down the checkered hall. Crazed Menoma-slaves in white, led by the insanely screeching Sultana, came behind. Out she went, out of the women's quarters; the group yelped after her like hounds chasing lox.

Sophie ran toward the dining halls hoping to gain the sizeable vegetable garden from the kitchens. She recalled a gate leading to a street from there—a way out of the palace, perhaps. She rushed through a dark and empty dining room and then past two fompa in a smaller room; they sat over lac tea and small glasses of schnapps and looked up in amazement as she passed by. The resplendent kitchen·was deserted—fortunately. She saw a door and ran into the garden. She heard Sultana's voice at high pitch; the woman was yelling at the fompa Sophie had left behind.

Sophie stopped outdoors, momentarily disoriented. She didn't recognize the garden from this vantage point and didn't have the time to look for that remembered gate. The sounds of gathering pursuit already reached her from the kitchen. She ran off into darkness and hid in a tool-shed under a pile of sacks.

She didn't stay there long. In a moment she heard the barking of a hound and knew that she would soon be caught by household guards. At least she had escaped Sultana and her murderous maidens.

The dog led the guards to her hiding place, and the guards took her away—an arm under each of her arms, a guard ahead, a guard behind—to Third Level, East Wing. A fompus waited at the entrance in the company of a gigantic slave; the slave had a greenish tint and a stupid sadness in his eyes.

"Come along," the fompus said and led the way along a narrow corridor with doors. Sophie followed; she glanced behind her from time to time; the giant slave hulked after her.

The fompus stopped at last before a door—a door in no way remarkable. Summoned by his gesture, the green man advanced, activated some mechanism set into the wall, and Sophie looked into a padded cell.

"In there," the fompus said. "Get in there and take off all your clothes. I mean it. If you don't do it willingly, he will do it for you.'' The fompus hooked a thumb toward the greenish man.

Sophie undressed. The fompus watched her. Goosebumps shivered across her skin—whether from his eyes or from the cold she couldn't say. He grunted some command; the green man entered to collect the clothes that she had laid on the rubbery floor.

"Good-bye for now," the fompus said. "Go ahead and go insane—if you like. We will get the facts out of your brain anyway, later, after the technicians come back.''

He offered no other comment or explanation; instead he motioned to the slave to leave the cell. The door closed with a rush, and Sophie was left alone in darkness.

She had spent most of her hours in that total, palpable darkness ever since. Once a day the green slave came to feed and shave her, and she had learned to like him—and to pity him. He belonged to a class of slaves used in high-security assignments. Unfortunates like her green Hulky received frequent injections of Menoma in certain regions of the brain to force them to forget specific things that they had seen or heard. Hulky would be dead within a month or so; no wonder that his eyes were sad.

Sophie felt that Hulky would soon come. She had developed the ability to predict his appearances.

Then the lights went on, startling her, as always. She closed and covered her eyes and listened for the door, for Hulky. He entered the cell carrying a tray of food and an electric razor and gave no reaction when she greeted him. She sighed. Then, without waiting a moment longer, she began to recite words and phrases she had thought up since the slave's last visit. She hoped that one of them would be the deep command to which the sad giant would react.

"Jump," she said. "Halt. At Ready. Now. Attention. I bid you. This instant." She paused briefly between phrases to see if he would go into receptivity, but Hulky remained untouched by her commands. He came to her and began to shave her; his razor slid against her skull humming and massaging her scalp.

"Baguse," she said. "Felina. Shima. Dog . . ." She continued to list animals; Hulky went on with his shaving. He didn't assume the rigid pose of receptivity.

She signed and began another litany. She found it more and more difficult to come up with appropriate words. The language seemed an inexhaustible well. Yet she knew that she had to persist; she knew there was a word or phrase to which he would respond. Sooner or later she would discover it and feared only that she might run out of time. One day the Contorti would return and Drusilla would then deal with her— permanently.

She went on and on. She grew breathless with haste and anxiety. Her skull was bare of hair. Hulky turned off the razor and moved slowly toward the empty food tray of the day before.

"Hulky," she cried, "don't go! Stay with me. Talk to me!"

He paid no attention to her plea. He bent to take the tray and activated the door with a key attached to his belt.

As the light suddenly vanished, Sophie broke into tears of frustration.

PART III

14 — INTERLUDE IN TYLUMPIN

The sun still hid below the line of the horizon, and early morning fog hung over Potsla Run. A young stable-boy moved toward the guest compound through the fog, a lampoon in his hand. It was so cold he shivered. He stopped before one of the houses and knocked on the door as he had been instructed to do—loud enough so that those inside would be aroused, gently enough so that others couldn't hear. Someone stirred inside and then a voice hissed, "Put out that light, you fool. We will be right out."

Balto and Jan emerged after a moment, each carrying a bag. They followed the boy over a crunching path made of white stones, past aromatic gardens each with its own trellised gazebo, and out to the road that divided Potsla Run into two halves. On the road they turned right and walked quickly toward the stables.

"Everything ready?" Jan asked.

The stable boy peered at him curiously. The voice was familiar, but this bearded fompus wasn't anyone he had ever met.

"Everything's arranged," he said, "just like the lord requested. We have a lac van waiting; the two animals are already loaded. A member of your household is here to drive the van. A guard."

Jan nodded. Leo had sent Fillip to drive them south.

Fillip was a technician and knew about such things as lac vans.

They saw the van before they arrived. It hovered off the ground ahead, its tail lights burning through the fog, a huge dirty levitator of the type used to carry lac blooms from South Bosom to the Simalta refineries. They would disappear in it unnoticed carrying Poruscht and Fleatcher.

Balto pressed a five-credit piece into the stable-boy's hand. Then he and Jan climbed into the cab. Shy, fat Fillip grinned in greeting and turned on the forward jets. Less than an hour later they had moved beyond Simalta and were climbing Crasnus by one of its three passes.

They arrived at the Tylumpin estate late in the morning. Leo stood before the handsome, columned mansion and smiled in welcome—a dignified, bearded man in a green turban, silver robe, red slippers.

After the animals were unloaded and stabled Leo gave them a short tour of the estate. "We will do a lot of walking in the next three weeks," he said. "The buildings are spread apart." But, he went on, the estate was ideal for a quiet stay. It was large, secluded, and well off any South Bosom highway—a hilly, wooded area. The ranch had an excellent, level spot for tafpa jousting. "It's screened on three sides by Nary pines," he said. "And the fourth side is a steep hill. Let me show you that first."

That field, with its dark pines all about exuding the aromatic Nary oils, that ground with its slightly uneven surface—it had been a plow-field some years back— became very familiar to Jan and Balto. They spent many hours there, usually alone, sometimes with members of the household as spectators. Here they worked, day after day, hour after hour. Jan on Poruscht impersonated Ignazio Contortus; Balto on Fleatcher impersonated himself. Each man wore leather armor and a visored helmet. They used touch-breaking lances for practice, and after some days a small pile of broken lances accumulated to one side of the field.

Not since his days on Potsla Run had Jan spent so much time on tafpa-back. The new routine did his soul good. He worked very hard with Balto and fell into his bed at night too tired to brood long over Sophie.

Nonetheless, he worried. Sophie had not appeared at the Fangano palace; there was no word of her. Fillip travelled to the Castle once a day to carry messages—and to inquire about Sophie; Leo used Fillip as a messenger to avoid the use of radio; Leo did not want to reveal his location in South Bosom, and Fillip, dressed in the uniform of the Castle Reserve and bearing a phoney pass, could serve as a surreptitious link between the family officials left up there and the household hiding in South Bosom. Radio silence seemed a good idea. Fillip brought word that Drusilla was frantic and that aircraft searched all over Fillippi looking for the Fanganos. Thus far none had overflown Tylum pin.

Each evening, at dusk, Jan walked out along the country road by which Fillip returned to the estate. Evening after evening Jan was disappointed when Fillip stopped the levitator and shook his head.

So time passed. Fillip travelled long distances every day and Jan trained Balto. The training went well; Jan was pleased with the results. At the outset he had told the lord: "If you can score against me four times out of ten, you can beat Ignazio. I'm a professional. I've spent years on tafpa back. The lance is like an extension of my arm."

Balto had achieved that goal. On some days, especially when Jan's concentration lagged, Balto's lance cracked against Jan's leather armor five, sometimes six times out of ten. One day, finally, Jan dropped his lance to the ground and slid off his tafpa.

"Lord," he said, "so far as I'm concerned, you're ready. You're good enough to get a job on Potsla Run."

Balto laughed in his deep, rumbling way. He pushed up his visor and wiped his sweaty face. "I hope that the next thing on the agenda is a week of rest. I lost four kilos in the last two weeks."

"Now that you can charge and hit, my lord," Jan said, "your basic training is done."

"But there's more, I suspect."

"Yes sir. Next I'll teach you how to take advantage of Glitsch's flaw."

Balto groaned in mock exhaustion.

They trained for some days more, and then the time ran out. During the last afternoon on Tylumpin estate they clashed lances one final time to demonstrate Balto's skill to Penta Mart; Mart had suddenly appeared on the estate. In the meantime the household bustled with activity. They were packing. Late that night, in accordance with a tight and finely tuned schedule, the household would descend on the Faltara Fair Grounds and occupy the space reserved for them.

Early that evening Jan walked out along the road which led from Tylumpin estate toward one of the South Bosom arteries. He would await Fillip once more, as he had done every morning. He saw no reason to change his ways just because this was the last day. Late tonight, after the move was completed, they'd establish radio communications with the household, and Fillip's trips could cease. It would be good to have the household in touch. But possibly, just possibly, Fillip would bring good news tonight.

He walked out, kicking rocks on the unpaved road. Yellow dust soon covered his boots. Lac fields lay to left and right; they extended for kilometers in both directions—golden yellow fields covered with a fine wire screen at the height of a man. The mesh had been erected to catch prematurely ripened blooms. As a rule the blooms were harvested before maturity, a week or so before they started levitating. Lac-farmers dressed in white cut them off the stem using the short-handled lacmordo while their women followed with vacuum hoses to suck up the precious blooms. Jan saw no farmers this evening.

He sat down on a stone to wait.

Mart had announced a council of war after dark and had included Jan as a participant—which pleased Jan no end. He was of the inner circle now; he could make a contribution and he wondered whether Mart would approve of an operation to free Sophie from the Contortus household—by force. Jan meant to suggest that tonight.

In a while Fillip gave the first sign of himself far away as a cloud of dust rising in the distance. Jan knew at once that Fillip brought no news. The floater came slowly, very slowly. Had Sophie arrived, Fillip would be racing as fast as the jets could push him.

When Fillip drew up, his jet reversing, Jan got in beside him without a word. Fillip's face revealed nothing, and Jan didn't ask the usual question.

They drove in silence. After a while Fillip turned to Jan.

"Don't take it so hard, Jan," he said. "In two days we will be the masters of Fillippi—then you can get her out of there yourself."

Mart held his meeting in one of the outlying farm-houses of Tylumpin, in the "big room" of the farm house. Dark beams criss-crossed the white-washed walls and ceiling. Skins lay on the floor. The men lounged on the skins in leisurely poses.

Mart squatted comfortably in the center and yet dis-played a certain tension, Jan thought, a readiness to act at a moment's notice. Now Mart concluded a short assessment of the situation, saying: "It looks like we've done everything we can do to win this joust."

"But not quite enough?"

"Not quite enough, Leo."

"In what respect?"

Mart shrugged. "I really blame myself, not any of you. Jan has done a terrific job of training. That busi-ness at the auction was also brilliant. And you, Balto," he bowed to the big man, "you have been a noble and diligent student. I liked what I saw out on the field today. But I still worry about Ignazio's luck."

Balto lay on the floor, his big hands behind his head. "We must score an unambiguous victory," he said. "We have to kill him early or wound him so severely that he refuses to go five rounds."

"If the joust lasts five rounds, we must kill him—not just wound him. We can't give his doctors a chance to patch him up. I don't know how they do it, but judging by the results of all the other duels, they must have medical knowledge not shared by the rest of the galaxy. I won't feel secure until I have better information. But time is running out."

"Since coming to this planet, I've become a Con-tortus watcher," Leo said. He stroked his beard. Un-like the others he sat on a chair. "The pattern of Ignazio's duels doesn't make sense to me. He is a clumsy, distracted, and cowardly man. Judging by physiognomy alone, he is not a man of the will, not a warrior at all.''

Mart nodded slowly. "I've thought about it a good deal myself, and I still think that they are using some sort of drug. Everything points to that. They must pump him full of some kind of hormone. Have you ever seen him in a duel?"

"I have," Balto said. "Once. And I know what you mean. He is fierce, bold, and resourceful—not at all like the man he seems to be."

"And he doesn't seem to suffer from his wounds," Leo added.

"Yes, that," Mart said. "And the drug—if it is a drug—must endow his body with a good deal of resistance. I've speculated at times that he is as listless and withdrawn as he is because the drug affects him."

"Which doesn't bother Drusilla at all," Leo said. "On the contrary!"

"Ignazio is a puppet. We all know that. But as Balto says, when he duels he is very fierce. He is a fierce puppet. I would like to do something about it, but I think it's too late. Even if we found out what drug they are using, we couldn't do anything about it, and here I'm thinking about some sort of antidote we could smear on the tip of your lance, Balto."

"The lance tips are analyzed for poison," Jan chimed in. "They will have their chemists over on our side, and our people will be over there."

"You're right," Mart said. "Nevertheless, if we knew something about the drug . . . The trouble is that I have never succeeded in getting an agent out of their palace alive. And this time I don't even have an agent in there."

"But we *do* have an agent in the palace," Jan cried.

He brought his quavering voice under control. "We have one in the household, but she can't seem to escape."

Mart swivelled on his haunches and turned full face to Jan. "What are you saying?"

"Jan's girl is in the Contortus household," Leo explained. Mart swivelled again, this time toward the fompus. "I haven't had time to brief you on that," Leo said. "And I'm not sure that she is an agent but she appears to have taken Phila and—"

"Any person who has taken Phila is an agent," Mart said with some intensity. He was clearly excited. "I wonder why I don't know about her." Mart swivelled toward Jan. "*Your* girl? The girl you were going to rescue that night I—kidnapped you?"

Jan nodded.

"Oh, Serendipity," Mart murmured. "And how is it that *you* know?"

Jan flushed. "It's a long story!"

"Out with it! Out with it!"

Jan blurted out his story in a few words, but Mart insisted on hearing all of it in considerable detail. Jan spoke for a long time while Mart listened with concentration, his eyes narrowed. He nodded at the end.

"So you think that she is still up there on Dominus?"

"Yes, sir," Jan said. "When we were in the palace, the household had already moved. That's the only reason Brudd went there."

Mart tapped a cheek with the flat of a hand for a moment. Then he made a wry expression and shook his head. "This sort of thing happens in every operation," he said. "If I had known about this, if I had known about a system of secret corridors—and where they meet the street . . . But—no matter." He turned to

Leo. "Do we have anyone reliable up there now—in your household?"

"Reliable yes," Leo said, "but not anybody senior."

"We need an officer up there," Mart said, "someone with Cush training."

"There is Fillip," Leo said. "He has been visiting up there every day. He's been our communications link while we had radio black-out."

"And Fillip knows Sophie," Jan said. "He was with me when Brudd dragged us into the palace."

Mart said, "I remember Fillip. Fat, shy boy. But reliable and tough when it counts."

Leo stroked his beard. "That's Fillip."

"Well, we'd better post him up there full time—just in case. When do you expect to have radio contact with the household?"

"After the move," Leo said. "By one or two in the morning at the latest."

"Tomorrow, then," Mart said. "Starting tomorrow, Fillip will be up there in case this girl shows up. She might have discovered something. And she might just escape."

Jan took a deep breath. "Couldn't we . . . couldn't we *do* something? Couldn't we try to get her out?"

Mart shook his head. "Sorry, Jan. I know what you're thinking, but now it's too late. It would require a massive operation, and we can't divert ourselves from the plan now. We must go ahead with plan and concentrate on the joust. And for the rest, we must simply trust to . . . luck." He reached out and boxed Jan playfully on the shoulder. "Don't worry. She'll be all right."

15 — THE SWEET TASTE OF INFORMATION

A few steps beyond the steel-tipped fence that encircled the Contortus complex, his own tent immediately behind him, Farnit Drusilla stood with arms folded and stared into the darkness. The night air carried a heavy scent of lac, the breeze from West Beach smelled of salt, and nature's mood was languid. But in the psychic ether around Drusilla information throbbed and danced. Inwardly the fompus was tense and excited. Out there, across the giant jousting field (the turf-covered center of Tent City), the Fanganos were moving in.

Drusilla had just dispatched another group of runners for more information. He had left his tent—where three visiphones and two radios kept him in touch with events—to see what he could see for himself. But it was too dark, and the jousting field too large. He could see almost nothing to the Fangano activity.

Nevertheless, Drusilla could imagine the scene out there. The Fangano transport chopper had landed after dark. Fangano guards had tumbled out even before the craft was anchored. They had thrown a ring around the Fangano territory, beamers in hand. A crowd of idlers had rapidly collected to watch the operation. Behind that bulwark of people, amidst erratically playing light beams, shouted instructions, and milling bodies, the

main Fangano tent was already halfway up. Its
sidewalls stood, but the center pole had not yet lifted
the peaked roof into the sky. The chopper had taken off
soon after landing to fetch another cargo, and Contortus
agents had determined its direction of travel: South
Bosom. Drusilla had always suspected that the Fanganos were hiding down there. A hastily dispatched
aerial reconnaissance team had reported a closed column of lac vans headed north—a Fangano convoy
loaded with the heavy gear.

Drusilla absorbed this information like a starved
man. Information. He hungered for every morsel. He
asked for and gulped down counts of people, generator
units unloaded, palace guards around the cordon, tents
staked out, and more, much more. Most of these
numbers were useless, but he wanted to know everything. He had to fill a gaping void of intelligence
created by weeks of silence.

After a moment in the dark, he grew restless and
turned back. He re-entered the complex of Contortus
tents through a steel-spiked gate. Then he was back in
his sparsely furnished tent again, surrounded by voices
and the crackle of static. He checked with his observers: Topper One and Two; Ludus One, Two, and Three;
and Skychief One. More data flowed into his brain and
lifted him higher. He exulted.

The tide has turned, he thought. The drift has
stopped. I'm in charge again.

In this frame of mind he looked up with annoyance as
the tent flap moved aside and a bald head looked in. The
sallow face, framed by outer darkness and lit by the dim
orange glow inside the spartan tent belonged to Sol
Teck's body servant.

"His lordship bids me to tell you that they're waiting
for you."

Let them wait. Three times the servant had come to fetch him; three times he would be sent back. Drusilla clicked off a radio on the small table. This creature had no need to overhear incoming traffic. He looked at the sallow face with distaste.

"Tell his lordship that I'll join them presently," he said. "Tell him I expect Captain Brudd any moment."

The man remained in the opening.

"Get out," Drusilla shouted in a sudden rage; and he hit the top of the small table with the flat of his hand. The head disappeared, and Drusilla turned to his radios again. He heard reports of the chopper's return. People and gear, once more. "Do you see Brudd?" he asked Topper One. Topper One observed the camp through infra-red binoculars from the branch of a tall papla behind the Fangano territory. The man hadn't seen Brudd. "Well, when you sight him I want an immediate report."

Drusilla rose from his seat and began to pace. His sandals sank into the padded canvas at every stilted step. The servant's appearance had released the poison of irritation. In thought he followed the bald messenger back from whence he came—to Ignazio's tent. Even now Solumnos Teck and others must be seated in a whispering circle around the Controller of Tundrati. And that quivering jelly ball no doubt sat there darkening in doubt.

We've come to that, Drusilla thought. Sol Teck has ready access to Ignazio. His voice openly competes with mine.

Cunning band, those Fanganos. They had denied him the intelligence he sought, data he needed to beat back Sol Teck's insinuations. Thousands of liters of hydrocarbon—imported at great cost from Herrarrium—had been wasted in the fruitless search. Brudd had been kept muzzled on some South Bosom farm. And by that cunning maneuver, Teck's power had been watered like a plant. Puny Teck had grown, grown, and grown. Well, now that was all over.

No, Drusilla thought, Sol Teck is not a poison herb. He's a disease germ. He relished the comparison. While the body is healthy and strong, the germ lies dormant in the tissue. Then at the first sign of weakness, it bursts into violent activity. But the disease isn't fatal; not yet. The process of decay can be reversed.

Over a number of weeks he had watched that process, impotent to stop it.

Important developments sometimes had tiny seeds. Sol Teck's power couldn't have flourished on Dominus, where Ignazio lived in seclusion. But on Faltara the Controller was more exposed. Here the family took its meal in a long, wide canvas banquet hall dominated by an immense ponok table of mirror-smooth surface. Old family custom demanded it—that the head of the family share dinner with the others on the islands. Ignazio abhorred the practice, but he followed it nevertheless. And there, at the communal board—Lord Cullu to his left, blowsy Csicsa on his right, Thamo, Fenid, Glamos, and Exume farther down—Ignazio was accessible.

Prompted by Teck who always sat behind him, Lord Cullu had begun to throw his poisoned darts soon after the move. Ignazio paid little attention to his uncle and ate as if he were alone. He kept his face over the bowl, and his hands worked fork and spoon with mechanical motions. From time to time he straightened up and signalled for more with a finger. Powdered "intimates" moved to fill up his plate. Then he would lower his pudgy face again to eat. But despite his outward indifference, he couldn't help hearing Lord Cullu's comments. They came with regularity one or two at every meal.

"I worry about your safety, Iggy," Lord Cullu would say. "Drusilla seems to have lost control." Then he would turn to Drusilla. "Your agent in the Fangano household hasn't told us much, has he? Where, by the way, are the Fanganos? Surely you know that much."

Drusilla had watched the process, day after day. He didn't have the crisp, factual answers to puncture these balloons of venom. Ignazio disregarded Cullu. He had a healthy hatred for the "Deep One." His uncle's gaunt features—those staring eyes, sunken cheeks, dark jowls, stiff, bristly hair—frightened the Controller. But slowly, slowly Cullu had penetrated.

"You must go see Huroka at his training, Iggy," he would say. "I'm no tafchuko myself, but I predict disaster."

Or—"Teck tells me that two of our 'friends' have broken their precious necks." A dry clicking of the tongue. "They can't stay up on that celebrated Glitsch. A hundred thousand credits we paid for him, imagine! Did you know that, Iggy? Sol says that we are the laughing stock of Concession. Glitsch had better be miraculously good on the field."

Or—"Of course you could resign, my boy. But then they would hound you to death—without the tundrati behind you. You've killed too many of their sons."

One day the Deep One had gotten through. Ignazio had turned his fat face to Drusilla. The eyes had looked out over their small ramparts of flesh. The red lips had trembled. "How bad is it, Farnit? Tell me honestly?"

And Sol Teck, who sat by the Deep One: "You'll forgive me this intrusion, lord, but the matter is grave.

We should discuss it in a formal meeting, not over food.''

"You may have to fight the joust yourself, Iggy, my boy. Huroka has said as much to me, but no one dares to tell you. I suppose Farnit will tell you the facts one of these days—but not until it is too late.''

Drusilla had risen on that occasion, his eyes flashing fire. "Nonsense! All this talk is nonsense. I have everything under control.''

Yet, Drusilla thought, recalling those conversations, he had lost control, control as he was used to it. Meetings had been called and, worse, meetings had been *held*. Shaken now, Ignazio had listened to the voices around him with unusual concentration. He had probed Drusilla's statements with unaccustomed vigor. Drusilla had fought back, fierce and bold as if he—not Ignazio—symbolized the felina. But his position had been difficult to defend. He had had no contact with his agent; he had still known nothing about Fangano motives; he had been as naked as a babe. Day by day his hold on Ignazio had slipped.

All that was over at last. Drusilla's channels of information were opening. He was back in the saddle again.

Drusilla stopped his pacing and activated a radio speaker. "Come in Topper One,''

"Topper here, chief.''

"Have you seen Brudd?''

"I might have, sir, but I can't be sure. It's total confusion down there. The chopper is lifting again. There is dust all over.''

"Ludus, Ludus One. Where *are* you, man. Why this damned silence?''

"Ludus, sir. The guards refuse to engage in conversation.''

''Well, then, send in those people in peasant dress. Maybe they'll talk to common folk. Dammit, Ludus, must I tell you everything? I want information on Brudd. Now.''

Over the crackling static of the radio, Drusilla didn't hear the swish of the tent flap. Nor, with his back to the entrance, did he see grizzled Colonel Lupus come in. The commander of the palace guard cleared his throat. Drusilla turned.

''Lupus,'' he said. ''I suppose Ignazio has sent you to fetch me in person.''

The colonel nodded.

''Very well, then, I'll go. Arrange for someone to monitor my traffic will you? Canfo or Filou or one of those men.''

The colonel nodded again.

Drusilla burst in upon the meeting, his eyes flashing with resolution. The meeting would be short, he told himself. Brudd could arrive at any moment to give his report.

He swept up an impression of the assembly with a single glance. All the dissidents were arranged around a central hassock in whose depths Ignazio brooded, a kitten on his lap. Huroka and Sol were to the left and right of the lord; next to them sat lesser fompa. All faced a screen on which Huroka had undoubtedly just shown films of the jousting practice.

''Here I am,'' Drusilla said. ''What do you want.'' He took up a stand by the entrance, near the screen; he folded his arms across his chest and arranged his face in a defiant expression. He sensed behind him, across the large oval of the jousting field, the Fangano move's hustle and bustle. It was pure information and it restored his sense of mastery.

Solumnos Teck had just removed his rimless glasses;

he moistened them with his breath and began to polish the lenses with the ample sleeve of his robe. He looked up—a precise, pedantic figure, his black hair parted in the center and pasted down with an oily tonic. People remembered the symmetry of his hair as they remembered Ignazio's streak. He spoke:

"We've been discussing options, Farnit," he said. "The films show that we're in trouble on the field. His lordship agrees that we can't go forward with the joust, and he has asked me to present some options. We thought you might want to sit in."

A week ago Drusilla would have felt impotent range, but now he was confident. He even felt a twinge of admiration for Teck's deft phrasing. In Sol's position Drusilla couldn't have done better himself. *He has asked me to present . . . you might want to sit in . . .* Outwardly Drusilla smiled. He set himself in motion and paraded up and down before the screen as he spoke.

"Our options," he said, gently lifting the initiative from Sol—(you've got a lot to learn yet, fompus, a lot to learn)—"the options I outlined to you the other day, Sol, are: one, to assassinate Balto. Two, to refuse the joust and to yield up our control of the tundrati. Three, to assume a military dictatorship. And four, to go forward with the duel. I hope you conveyed those choices to Ignazio as I've laid them out."

"Pardon me, Farnit, but—"

"Which I'm sure you did," Drusilla said, raising his voice, overriding Teck. He was pleased that Cullu was absent. The Deep One would have stopped this charade. Against Sol Teck, man against man, with Ignazio as judge and jury, Drusilla could prevail by sheer force of will. "I hope you've also told Ignazio the serious misgivings you voiced to me about the first three options."

"Your lordship, Farnit is—"

"Which were—if you'll permit me to finish, very real objections. I hope you haven't kept them to yourself. You must be as candid with Ignazio as you are with me and Lord Cullu."

"Farnit, I can't just sit here and let you bully me—"

"My lord," Drusilla cried, fixing the pudgy figure with his eyes, "can I be permitted to finish without interruptions?"

"Let him finish," Ignazio said from the depths of the hassock. He avoided Teck's eyes as he spoke.

"Very well," Drusilla continued. He sensed his own new-found confidence. It radiated toward Ignazio and rang in the sharp clarity of his voice. Ignazio's puffy eyes relaxed as they turned to the chief fompus who was, once more, truly *chief* fompus. All that information pulsed behind him and made him bold.

"Sol has misgivings, which I share," he said. "Balto's assassination will yield a rash of challenges. Sol reminds us that the lords are restless. We've had another movement to revise the Constitution. An assassination could tilt the balance against us. It could result—why, we might have thirty lords challenge you, Ignazio, all at once. We couldn't assassinate them all, nor could Huroka handle that load. He as much as admits he can't stage a single tafpa joust. What about ten? What about twenty?"

"With all due respect, your lordship, I have never made that argument, nor would I. It's preposterous." Sol Teck's voice quavered with indignation.

"You should have, Teck," Drusil'a said. "You should have. Twenty jousts, Ignazio. Think of that. And turning to the second and third options—they will invite assassination—yours, Ignazio. Yours. For all

intents and purposes you're already dictator of Fillippi.
But you hold your power legally under the constitution.
Why jeopardize it? If you resign, you invite vengeance.
Lord Cullu has explained that very aptly over dinner the
other night. Too many families have accounts to settle.
Which leaves us with the final option; fight the joust.
You don't have to win it, as I've explained a hundred
times. All you have to do is fight it. Fight and you
remain in power, and your power is legally yours.
That's where I come out.''

"Your lordship, with due respect, may I have a turn
to speak?"

"Speak away, Sol," Drusilla cried, the initiative
tightly in his hands. "Speak away, but keep it short.
Captain Brudd just told me a few things that I must
discuss with Huroka. It appears he can do much for us.
With Brudd on the other side, even our 'friends' have a
good chance to win."

"Brudd here?" Huroka rasped in surprise.

"Here and gone again," Drusilla lied. 'He slipped
away. He couldn't stay very long. They're unloading
tafpas now on the other side of the field."

"Your lordship, Farnit is deliberately leading us
from the subject of the meeting. I must have leave to
speak."

Drusilla said: "You're speaking, Sol. Please con-
tinue."

Teck disregarded Drusilla's permission. He turned
to address the lounging Controller. "Your lordship,
Farnit's last option is perhaps more dangerous than any
of the others. I've taken pains to remind you how tafpa
jousts are fought. The event is in the open, watched by
hundreds of people. The lances are thick, wooden
beams—one could almost call them poles. They're
tipped with steel. Tafpa speeds are enormous in the

volta, and the shock of collision can be explosive.
Anything can happen. The lance can tear off a head, an
arm, or it could go right through the chest. Have you
ever seen a blood joust, lord?''

"I have and I'm not worried," Drusilla said. "The
probabilities are low that something like that will happen.''

Now Ignazio stirred. He pulled himself out of the
soft concavity his body had formed in the soft hassock
and sat on its edge. He rested his stubby arms on thick
tights. The kitten slipped from his lap and stalked
away.

"What Teck says worries me too, Farnit. The lance
could tear off the head. And suppose it rolls several
meters from the body. What do we do then?''

It was clear from Ignazio's nauseous expression that
he saw the scene in his mind's eyes—his head, his
features, his streaked hair rolling . . . rolling . . .
rolling on the ground with a wibble and a wobble over
the pudgy nose.

"Improbable, highly improbable," Drusilla said.
"For that matter a meteorite could drop on our
'friend's' head too. I've never seen a head roll at a
joust.''

"Your lordship, it could happen.''

"Anything could happen, Sol. I will grant you that.
Did you know that only five blood jousts in ten are
fatal? The chances for disaster are low. We might very
well win.''

"Not with our 'friends'," Huroka threw in, de-
jected. "They look sick. I told you all at the beginning,
I warned everyone . . .''

Drusilla gave the rat-faced man a contemptuous
glance. "You won't be held responsible, Huroka. But
neither will you get credit for success. The credit will

go to Brudd—for the help he will render us from the other end. And the credit will go to you, Ignazio—for courageous decisions from start to finish.''

One of Drusilla's aides had stuck his head through the tent flap and had waited for the chief fompus to finish. Now he gestured to Drusilla with an expression of urgency.

"Just a minute, Filou. Wait for me outside.''

Drusilla turned back to the assembly. He gestured toward the tent flap. "As you can see, my lord, I'm in the midst of an operation. The Fanganos are moving in. Our agents are swarming all over their camp. I can't waste time listening to prophets of doom. All the signs are positive now. Brudd is there in the midst of the enemy, and he will do things for us between rounds to disorganize Balto and his people. I am absolutely certain that we shall succeed.''

He glanced around the room again.

"Have you heard enough? Or do we go on with the conversation. We're wasting time.''

He waited, eyes fixed on Ignazio. The pudgy lord squirmed, clearly in great discomfort.

"Sol,'' the Controller said at last, "I believe you asked for this meeting. Are you satisfied?''

Teck removed his spectacles. "I'm satisfied if your lordship is. Huroka here felt that your lordship should know what you're facing. We've all seen the films. Farnit seems very sure of himself, for a change, and we all hope that he is right. Much here rides on his judgment, lord, perhaps too much. For that very reason, I thought it worth-while to explore options.''

Sol Teck is hedging his bets, Drusilla noted. If something goes wrong, I'm alone. He blames the meeting on Huroka. He frees Ignazio of all responsibility. Clever of him.

Filou's head appeared through the flap again. "Fompus," he hissed, "it's urgent."

Drusilla nodded to his agent and waved him out. Filou was the over-eager type.

"Your concern for his lordship is touching," he said, turning to Teck. "Touching but totally unwarranted. I'm sure Ignazio will agree that I've given him accurate assessments of the situation all along."

"I didn't question that," Teck said. "But in my role as your deputy, I felt it would be meaningful to explore alternatives."

"After the joust," Drusilla said, spinning a not-too-veiled threat, "we must assemble again for a retrospective view. You seem to enjoy having meetings, Sol. It may be instructive, after the event, to see how my strategy worked out."

"As you know, Farnit, I fully support his lordship's decisions."

Drusilla turned to Ignazio. "I take it then, Ignazio, that your original decision still stands? We go forward as planned and don't indulge in speculation until it's necessary?"

He didn't wait for a response. "That will be all, gentlemen. I suggest we all turn now to more constructive activities." He waited before the screen, arms folded across his chest. He waited, clearly, for everyone to leave. The assembly rose slowly. Only Ignazio remained sunk back in his hassock. The others filed out, their expressions gloomy with defeat. Left alone with the lord, Drusilla now turned to him.

"I didn't want this meeting, my friend," he said, his tone openly aggressive. "But you insisted. The next time you overrule me, especially in the middle of a crisis, remember this—without me the Contorti are nothing. Remove me at your peril, lord."

He turned and immediately left. Ignazio remained sunk in his soft leather, an embarrassed, pained look on his face.

"What is it, Filou?"

"Fompus, we've just had a report. Brudd's not with the party."

"How do you know that? In this darkness and confusion, who can be sure?"

"One of their servants told it to one of our observers, one of those dressed in peasant dress you told Ludus One to send in. 'We left him up on Dominus. He has an important job to do up there.' Those were the words."

"Damnation," Drusilla said evenly. He stared, thinking. Then he turned to Filou. "Get me Colonel Lupus at once. Tell him to meet me in my tent. Don't whisper a word of this to anyone, or I'll put your head in your lap."

16 — "HUROKA!"

In the Contortus Palace, some hours later, in a small cell in Third Level, East Wing, Sophie awoke in a state of unnatural excitement, but the excitement yielded rapidly to a feeling of calm serenity. Days, weeks, possibly even months had passed since her imprisonment; at times she had lost all sense of time and at times she had tottered on the verge of madness; but now clarity and certainty had returned, and she felt herself in the presence of the real Sophie again—the sure, deliberate, and competent person that she was.

This pleasant sensation came from an inner certainty that she had found the word at last, that word. She had absolutely no doubt about it. The word had come to her in sleep; she had awakened with it on her lips.

"Huroka."

She had whispered the word to herself upon awakening, unsure for a moment why; then it had all sorted out, and she felt now what at times she had felt in Tesso meditation—a harmonious emptiness, a still knowing.

Smiling to herself in the darkness, she recalled the thousands of words she had tried on Hulky—recalled the string of disappointments. Somehow she had tried too hard. In her anxiety and eagerness to get away, she had overlooked the obvious. East Wing was Huroka's realm. His name had to be the trigger word, the key to the subconscious mind of the slaves. The same key would open the cell door.

She turned her thoughts to practical matters. She would need clothing of some kind and a hat to hide her shaven head. What else? She guessed that her notebooks had been found by now. She had no need for them in any event; her activities as an agent had been interrupted before she could find that certain "pattern"; the best thing she could do now was to get away. But where? Then she remembered Jan's words. She could try to find the Fangano household in the Southwest District, the family whose emblem was the platypus, whose fompus was called Leo. It amazed her that she still remembered Jan's instructions after all the confusion, disorientation, and all those many other words . . .

A little later the light went on and greenish sad-eyed Hulky came in. He carried a tray and razor, as usual, and again, as usual, he didn't look at Sophie. She observed him with new interest, however, and noted that he wore a pair of simple pants and sandals. The pants would do for a start, but Sophie wished that Hulky was wearing a shirt. She suppressed her excitement, and before the giant could shut the door, she called out the word, not too loudly, not too softly.

"Huroka," she said.

She saw with a thrill that she had hit the mark this time. Hulky's sad eyes glazed over immediately; he froze; he was "receptive".

"You will do exactly what I say," she said. "Can you talk?"

Hulky shook his head.

"Take off your pants and give them to me."

He did so, and she slipped into the huge garment

immediately. Even adjusting the elastic left the trousers too loose, but at least they covered some of her nakedness; she couldn't very well run about these halls entirely naked—as in a bad dream. She bent down to roll up the trouser legs. Then she straightened and turned toward her slave.

"How many servants on this floor?"

Hulky held up three fingers.

"Are they all like you?" He nodded. "Are there any fompa here?" He shook his head. "Where are the fompa?" He stared; he couldn't respond to that. "Are the fompa sleeping?" He nodded. "Is it night time?" Yes. "How many palace guards are here?" He shook his head. "No palace guards?" He nodded. "Are you sure of that? No guards?" He nodded. "Where are they?" But he just stared.

"Never mind," she said. "I want you to turn around and face the wall. I am going to leave now, and you will forget that I left. You will stay in this cell until someone gets you. If you get sleepy, you may lie down to sleep."

Hulky turned toward the wall, and Sophie stepped to the door. Carefully, she peered out to assure herself of unobserved passage and saw an empty hall bathed in dim overhead light. She was about to leave but turned back on an impulse. She ran to Hulky and pecked a kiss on the green giant's cheek from behind. "Good-bye, Hulky," she said. "May the Way bless you." Then she left hurriedly and ran out on naked tip-toes down that empty corridor.

In a moment she arrived at the intersection with another corridor and stopped in breathless excitement, unsure which way to go.

I must be totally in control, she told herself, entirely deliberate.

Deliberately, she turned toward the right and soon found herself rewarded. She had left the area devoted to cells of the sort in which she had resided for days or weeks or even months and found herself in some sort of administrative area. Very carefully at first, then with growing assurance, she opened a succession of doors and saw offices, store rooms, lavatories, and several rooms filled with shelves. She had seen such rooms in the Tower and knew that the oblong boxes on the shelves contained Menoma tapes. The Contorti were training slaves on something like a grand scale up here. She poked into drawers and looked into cabinets, but nowhere did she find the least shred of clothing.

In the next corridor—she had turned right again— she found other types of facilities, each puzzling. Swords and daggers hung on the walls of one room, and a long rubber mat ran the length of it. She fingered fencing masks on a table but decided that they wouldn't do for a hat. In another room she saw all manner of athletic equipment—weights, treadmills, bicycles. Next door was a shooting gallery with beamers stacked neatly in racks, lead vests clustered on rows of hooks, and charred targets high up on a kind of stage. Yet another room had mock-ups of a chopper's controls and of a speedboat's wheel; screens above each mock-up suggested that these were simulators. She wondered vaguely what all this meant, but her mind was on the search—for a skirt, a blouse, a hat.

Then, up ahead, she saw double doors; they blocked off the corridor; in big red letters on their shiny white surface stood the words PLASTIC SURGERY, KEEP OUT.

Surgery? Surgery might mean white coats, white hats, and other medical paraphernalia. She advanced toward the doors still thinking about dress—Hulky's pants protected her no more than a barrel might—and didn't even wonder why deep inside the Contortus palace plastic surgery might be practiced in such a large facility.

The area she entered now resembled a hospital. The odor of medicines hung in the air, machinery throbbed somewhere, and all the walls and surfaces were meticulously clean. She passed laboratories and examination rooms and spaces crowded with gleaming instruments whose purposes she could not divine. She opened closets and pulled out drawers certain that she would find what she was looking for—decent coverings for her nakedness.

About midway in this medical complex, she saw yet another door and opened it—and immediately shut it again in fright. Her heart raced and she almost dashed away, but something held her in place. She had glimpsed *people* inside that room, several people lying on beds, identical people! And they had been sleeping. But who were they? She knew the face—the one face they all had—but now the name escaped her.

She remembered suddenly that she was a member of Cush, an agent on assignment. Those sleepers beyond the door carried some secret she had to uncover even at the risk of being apprehended. She had another reason to enter as well: she thought she had seen tundratus uniforms draped over chairs at the foot of each bed.

She opened the door very slowly, just a crack, and peered inside. After a moment she went in, no longer fearful of apprehension.

Ten beds stood in the room to her left, five of them empty. In the other beds lay five men. Each one bore the unmistakable likeness of Ignazio Contortus. She recognized him now and also knew why she hadn't done so right away. All five men were bald. Elaborate wigs, each with the blond streak running down the center, lay on the chairs over red tundratus tunics.

Sophie stood and stared in some amazement. These likenesses of the famous Contortus slept the unnatural sleep of conditioning, their naked skulls pasted with electrodes, electrodes linked by wire to a bank of tape machines suspended from the ceiling. Remembering that she was still an agent—and in excited pleasure at her discovery—she approached one of the Ignazios and leaned down over the chubby face. Faint, almost invisible traces of scar tissue marked the lines where some poor Menoma slave had been altered by plastic surgery, by the knife of the surgical sculptor. Had Huroka made these likenesses?

She shuddered and turned away.

Minutes later she left the room transformed in appearance. Her hair was long and black and sported the fashionable central streak. She wore the red tunic of a regular tundratus and black trousers tucked into boots. She was all set to go.

Down the hall she turned right again, and then again. And then she saw ahead a door marked HEAD SURGEON. She entered it and found herself inside a large and ornate office. She noticed at once that one of the walls was decorated with carved panels. She approached the wall, looking for a gargoyle with metallic eyes.

She recognized the Fangano palace by the platypus carved into the headstone above the column-supported entrance and was pleased to see lights from windows of all three stories of the building. The Fanganos were still up—despite the lateness of the hour. Sophie guessed that a festival of some kind must be in progress. She mounted the steps, passed between sturdy columns, and rang the bell.

The door opened partially in a moment and a palace guard in tundratus uniform looked out. Bright lights behind him converted his head and trunk into a silhouette.

"Well, well," he cried. "What do we have here? A young soldier with a fancy hairdo, that's what. A late-comer. Where have you been? Whoring on Third Level? Get in here with you."

With sudden vehemence and a change in expression, the guard opened the door all the way, grabbed her arm, and pulled her rudely from the darkness into a dimly lit front hall. His tone and manner alarmed her and put her on her guard. She took in the interior, and what she saw frightened and froze her. She had escaped the frying pan only to land in the fire.

Three large entries opened from the hall into the interior rooms of the palace. Wide speckled marble steps led from the low-lying foyer where she stood to the rooms. She saw tundrati in those rooms, some armed, some not. They gave her the impression of a loose, marauding band. Two soldiers played catch with crystal-ware and roared in childish glee whenever a piece dropped to the marble floor and shattered. A group played dice on the floor, drinking wine from bottles that had been opened with beam-gun stocks. Two men tossed knives at an oil painting and tried to hit the droll, heavy-set marsupials shown on the paintings. A man was urinating on the floor . . .

All of the men wore on their lapels the "leaping felina," emblem of the Contorti. The guards from the Contortus palace whose whereabouts Hulky had been unable to explain were here!

"You were plain lucky," the guard said. "You might have been here when we attacked. Most of your buddies are dead. I'd just as soon kill you as not—if it weren't for a deep command. Drusilla wants to question all of you in person. Then *we* will get to play with you. VULTUS," he shouted, "here is another one for the cellar. Get along with you, Fangano baguse."

With that he shoved Sophie forward violently and kicked her brutally from the back. She stumbled toward a small door which also opened into the hall. There a surly soldier now appeared.

"Come along," he said. He went ahead, rattling keys on a large ring. Sophie limped after him, her left leg numb from the kick. The soldier took no interest in her, which was just as well. She had thinned out enough during her imprisonment to pass for a young man—but not on close examination. She smelled ozone mixed with smoke from something that still burned. The Fangano palace had been the scene of a recently-fought beamer battle.

Suddenly the implications of that battle burst in upon her. Jan might be dead. *Most* of your buddies are dead, the soldier had said. Then Jan might still be alive! But in any event, Cush must have been discovered and put down—which meant that both of them were lost!

They went down narrow stone stairs in a spiral—around and around and around a central post.

Sophie took herself in hand. Tesso had written: "You are spirit, pure and simple. Pure, unsullied substance—indestructible, indivisible, and One." She was spirit and spirit stood above the manifestations of the world.

How far down did these stairs reach? They went down and around and around. Their boots made hollow sounds on the stone.

I don't know enough about the situation to judge it, she told herself. I don't *know* that Cush is crushed or that Jan is alive or dead. I must wait patiently.

They reached the botton, and the soldier turned left. She smelled levitron. They were at least on Level Three, maybe on Level Four. They passed heavy wooden doors closing off vaulted entries. He stopped before one and selected the key. The door creaked as he opened it.

"In you go," the surly soldier said, and he pushed her forward, into darkness.

17 — OTHER CAUSES AND DUBU-DAM-DAM

I remember Fillip. Fat, shy boy. But reliable and tough when it counts.

—*Penta Mart*

When Fillip jumped out of the Faltara-Dominus shuttle craft, it was around eleven in the morning. Nonetheless he felt very tired. Overlaying his fatigue was an artificial alertness caused by expectation of adversity.

He walked across the airport's stone-covered runway to the terminal building, buttoning his tundratus jacket as he went. He wore the emblem of the regular communications corps on his lapels.

He told himself to be alert and watchful. The communications failure of the night before could have mechanical causes. Or "other causes." He had to be on his guard in case he ran into Other Causes.

At the gate he showed his pass, the genuine article encased in tamper-proof plastic. It identified him as a member of the Castle reserve and as a courier. The guards already knew him and waved him through after perfunctory glances at his papers. He passed out of the terminal through self-opening doors and headed south.

He had worked half the night erecting the Fangano tents at the fair grounds. They had installed the communications equipment late at night and had checked it out, but the Fangano palace had not responded, not on any channel. Fillip had tried to reach the boys up there for better than an hour. Then Leo had put a stop to it.

"Go to sleep, Fillip," he had said. "You will go up tomorrow in any event; you can look into it then. Most of us are down here, and it's not critical that we have communications."

Fillip reached the Outer Circumferential and turned west, toward the Fangano palace.

The joust would begin tomorrow, twenty-four hours from now. He would be up here in the company of two or three old servants and a handful of palace guards. Meanwhile the most exciting event in fifty years of Fillippi history would be enacted down below. It made him want to cry.

Mart had told the group that he had trained with, "We must serve where Cush sends us. We mustn't question our assignment. We are like the cells of a single body, and whatever we do is useful."

The noble words had thrilled him then. He had liked the sound of that. He had never been ambitious and had always preferred obscurity. But there was a limit. He would be sitting on his hands up here, and if the radio was on the blink he wouldn't even know the outcome of the joust.

He judged the probabilities very low that Jan's girl would show up, although he prayed that she would—for Jan's sake.

He neared the palace and unbuttoned his jacket. The walk had made him hot. His gloom blew away now that he was near. Curiosity replaced his chagrin and he wondered why the palace had failed to respond during the night and again this morning. If the radio was down, he would have something to do. He liked to fuss with complex equipment; the diagnosis and cure of mechanical diseases was his longest suit.

One street away from the Fangano palace he turned off the Circumferential. Instinct nudged him to be careful and to approach the palace unannounced. He thought about Other Causes and meant to check a little before he rang any bells.

A side street took him to an alley paralleling the Circumferential and here he negotiated a wrought iron fence, crossed the gardens of a neighboring palace, and reaching a high wall the Fanganos had erected to secure their privacy. He stood before that wall for a moment, listening, than he braced himself for the difficult climb up the rough surface made of stones set in carelessly slapped mortar.

He rolled over the top of the wall and fell down into a garden behind the Fangano palace secure in his mind that he could not have been observed. Balto's uncle raised plants and flowers from Felicitas in this aromatic space, and the alien growths, evolved over eons in much greater gravity, grew thickly and luxuriously here; they hid the palace from Fillip's view. He rested for a moment on hands and knees, listening, listening. Then, cautiously, he made his way toward the complex of Fangano buildings between odd, elongated plants and trees that swayed, heavy with pods and hexagonal blooms, eight, ten, twelve meters in the air.

In a moment he saw the central building, went down on hands and knees, and crawled forward slowly using a line of bushes as his screen. He spied on the building from the shade of those bushes, and soon forgot all about the Faltara joust. He had guessed correctly about Other Causes and knew that he would have his hands full right here on Dominus.

The broken windows had drawn his attention first.

There he glimpsed broken furniture on the tiny lawn behind the palace; some of those objects had been hurled through the windows. Broken china littered the back. Many of Harom's elongated plants and shrubs had been cut down or burned by beam-guns. A small fountain lay on its side; a fat nymph lay next to it without a head.

Apart from these signs of vandalism, Fillip saw no sign of life. The only movement came from a mournful lace curtain blowing in the breeze through a broken window.

He had seen enough, and withdrew a ways to make a plan.

Two hours later he approached the palace again, this time by an entirely different route. He came toward the palace through one of the dim maintenance ducts of Third Level. He walked in a stink of levitron and carried gear he had "requistioned" from a maintenance cubicle.

A massive door marked the point where the public space ended and the Fangano palace began. He laid his implements on the floor and began to work on that door using a beam cutter. He cut a circular hole around the lock. It was slow, sweaty work; the metal was thick, the beam-cutter designed for light-weight work. Wild sparks flew about, the metal flowed, and Fillip coughed and cursed in the dark, smoke-filled place. At last his ragged circle was completed; the lock fell in, and the door opened slowly at his touch.

He stood at the end of a long, dark corridor. The beam of his flashlight revealed arched doorways on either side closed off by heavy wooden portals. He smiled with satisfaction; he had entered at the very point where he had hoped he would—the Fangano storage cellar.

He had come in this way for two reasons. He expected no opposition down here in the stinking dungeons of Third Level. And he hoped to find a weapon here. Some weeks ago young Tullo Fangano, Balto's teenage son, had told Fillip about some sporting guns stored in the cellars. Those curious implements had never been used on Fillippi, Tullo had said. Balto had used them as a boy to hunt the heavy beasts of Felicitas. The guns had made an impression on Fillip at the time because they had a curious name. Tullo had called them *Dubu-dam-dams*. They were primitive pellet projectors and made loud sounds when fired—hence the name.

Fillip had his doubts about the usefulness of *dubu-dam-dams* in an honest-to-goodness fight, but he had come unarmed, and any weapon would be better than none at all.

Now he looked at all those wooden doors and wondered which might hold the guns.

Systematical by nature, he rejected a random search. He would take each storage room in turn. He let his cutter cool for a while and then attacked the first door. The lock yielded readily. Three or four bursts from the tool, a flash of sparks, and the door opened with a creak. Soon he was hard at work, moving from room to room. And it was dull work. He saw and poked through centuries of accumulated family treasures kept for sentimental reasons. Most of the stuff was worthless. It was also very slow work; he had to search each room thoroughly. He opened crates of the appropriate size and lifted and looked under everything. Of all the objects he came across he took only

two: an old lead vest and face shield; they might be
useful if he ran into beamers.

It was late afternoon when he opened the twelfth
door and saw the weapons directly in front of him,
neatly placed on a rack—old-fashioned projectile
weapons made of steel and wood. They were enormous in size; almost as high, with the butt on the floor,
as Fillip was tall. He found ammunition in boxes:
thick, blunt bullets for heavy game. He sat down to
inspect the unfamiliar mechanisms.

As he played with the guns, he heard again what he
had heard at intervals before—a dull, rhythmic pounding noise. He couldn't place the origin of the sound. It
appeared to vibrate through the walls. He planned to
investigate that sound, by and by, but now he was eager
to move upstairs to see what damage had been done.

Suppose no one is here, he wondered, and I spent my
day searching for nothing. He shrugged. Better safe
than surprised.

He selected one of the guns and (to be on the safe
side, to be conservative), he loaded himself with suitable ammunition. He put on the lead vest and the face
mask and took off his boots. Then, silently, he moved
toward a spiral staircase that led to the regions above.

From all appearances the house stood empty. He
reached street level without encountering a soul.
Through broken windows he saw that dusk had set in.
Sirica gleamed in the sky, Fillippi's evening star. He
moved through the kitchen complex stepping over debris. This place had been ransacked by professionals.
He made for the front rooms. He had to pass through
them to reach the communications center on the other
side of the mansion.

The dining hall was such a shambles that he lost his
concentration for a moment and inadvertently kicked a

broken clay urn. It rolled a ways with a dull crackling sound.

Immediately he heard a voice.

"Vultus, Gabriello? Is that you? I heard a noise in the kitchen."

Fillip took cover behind a heavy over-turned credenza. Its contents had spilled and littered the marble floor of the dining hall.

He heard boots running over marble. From the sound he judged these to be tundratus boots. He noted that the Fangano household had no guards named Vultus or Gabriello.

The same voice spoke again, much nearer. Fillip judged it to be next door, toward the garden side, in the small sitting room.

"Vultus, fetch Tanus and Carpo," the voice said, more muffled now; the man had put on a face mask. "Then let's go in together. This place makes me feel creepy, now that the others are gone."

Steps receeded.

Fillip sweated. What should he do? He counted. He had heard the man call four names. If there were only five here, he must attack. This damnable weapon was a sporting gun. You had to load it after every shot. If only he had a beamer. He could cut them all down in a single pass provided he could get a shot at their unshielded legs.

He peered over the upper edge of the credenza. They would come in through that opening on the right. His view was obscured somewhat by a couch turned on end. The heavy dining table lay on edge, its legs pointing toward him. He couldn't shoot at their legs, he saw. The table blocked him. Too bad.

Do you suppose this gun can shoot through a centimeter of lead? Not bloody likely.

Tundratus boots came running.

He had to take a chance. He would have to let them all into the room, then shoot and load as fast as he could. He looked behind him to ensure he had a retreat.

The lights went on. Fillip peered between the edge of the credenza and the couch standing on its end.

He saw a felina emblem. Contorti. So Contorti had attacked. But why? Maybe to rescue Brudd? They had attacked and used vandalism as a cover. Such things happened when the lords were down on the islands.

All this flashed through his mind in a single thought, even as he noted that the men were armed and shielded. They moved very slowly. He let them come in. They had nearly reached the upturned table when he rose and fired. The gun's recoil almost threw him down, his shoulder badly wrenched. His ears sang with the unexpected, shattering blast.

Fillip had aimed at the man in the center. The man spun backwards and dropped against the wall face first. The bullet had torn a hole into his back as it had passed through him.

God of the Cosmos! This gun went through lead like a knife through cheese.

His fingers fumbled, inserting a bullet. He didn't recognize the pungent odor of the blast.

He crawled rapidly to the other end of the credenza. Above him gun beams flickered and burned circles in the wall. He could feel the intense heat and smelled ozone. Someone shot out the light and the room was plunged into semi-darkness.

He peered around the far edge and took aim. The soldiers lay behind the heavy table now, and he couldn't take aim at much—but from this angle, he noted, he could control the door.

He pressed the stock against his aching shoulder and squeezed the trigger.

A yell of anguish! Wood splinters flew. Then beams found his corner of the credenza, and he had to withdraw.

Crawling back he noticed a gun beam directed at the hinge of the kitchen door behind him. The hinge glowed red. It would give way in a second. He sought an angle for a shot, but two guns now searched every possible edge of the credenza. They were wasting power, but no doubt they were desperate. His gun could penetrate lead and might even wound through the heavy wood of the table.

The door crashed down behind him.

He admired their tactics from a strictly military viewpoint. The door now blocked his retreat. He could jump over it, but he would expose himself to fire.

Back at the far end of the credenza he slipped off his lead vest. He found a table knife on the floor and with it he slowly forced an opening through the fabric and the metal and pressed the barrel of his gun through that opening. Then he peered out, just in time to see a man crawling for the door.

He prepared to shoot. Beams beat against the exposed part of his face mask, but the lead protected him.

"Back, Vultus, back," a voice shouted.

The warning came too late. Fillip's sporting artillery exploded again, and Vultus rolled against the door jamb, dead.

I'm pinned down, Fillip thought. But then again, so are they.

18 — THE JOUST

Hit, hit, hit, hit!
      —Crowd cheer at tafpa jousts

"Still no radio communications. Fillip has been up there for a day—and still no word. Do you think I should send some of our people up?"

Leo stood outside the entrance of the main Fangano tent. He was neat and fresh in a turban and a silver robe despite a sleepless night.

Balto shook his head. "No," he said, over his shoulder. Leather breast-plates covered his massive chest. Behind him Jan tightened straps that held the plates in place.

"No," Balto said again, "I'm convinced that this is a diversion. They want to shake our concentration."

"I will keep trying," Leo said and ducked back into the tent.

Balto and Jan were in a frontal hall area protected from view by canvas walls, but this portion of the Fangano complex had no roof, and they could see clouds racing overhead against the sky. Through an opening they could see milling servants readying Fleatcher for the joust.

"That should do it," Jan said. "Move about, twist and bend. You must be comfortable."

Balto went down on his haunches, rotated his trunk, and swung his arms. Then he pounded the leather plates with fists as if they were drums.

"Not much protection against that lance tip," he said.

"It's not supposed to be," Jan said. "The ancients used to ride naked in the blood joust. 'Clothed safety round in courage alone,'" Jan quoted. "All right. Let's put on your leg shields."

"Listen to them," Balto said while Jan fitted and then tightened oblong half-tubes of leather around Balto's thighs and shins.

The crowd hummed and roared like the surf on a stormy day.

"They started coming before dawn," Jan said, straining. "Drusilla threw a cordon of Gash tundrati around the fair grounds, but they've slipped in somehow anyway. There must be thousands of them—men, women, old ladies, children. There you go." He slapped Balto's calf indicating that the operation was finished.

"Ten minutes," cried a young boy at the entry to the outer courtyard. He disappeared again.

"Better slip into your robe before you put your arm plates on."

The half-robe hung over a canvas chair, a green silk garment embroidered with the platypus emblem in white thread. Balto slipped it over his head. It had no arms. He gathered the waist into a wide, stone-studded belt and pulled down on the fabric so that it formed an even skirt beneath his waist.

"Arm plates," Jan said. "Don't tighten them too much."

"I will feel naked without a helmet," Balto rumbled.

"No helmets in blood jousts," Jan said. "But at least you'll see the terror on Ignazio's face when he gets hit."

"Let's hope," Balto said.

Leo came out of the tent again. "The Senate has arrived," he said. "All of them are in the box now, from Fantidaimi on down. There is much more than a quorum."

"Good," Balto said. "Jan, I can't get this clip loose."

Jan stepped over to help him.

"Balto," the fompus said. His voice revealed a hesitation and embarrassment. "I—"

Balto turned.

"You'll be out there in a few minutes," the fompus said, "and this is probably our last chance to talk. I—I wanted to say to you . . . Balto, Felicitas would be proud of you today." His eyes moistened. "God be with you, old friend." He reached out and clasped Balto's big hand. Then he turned and disappeared.

The clips were adjusted, and Balto was ready.

"Remember now, my lord. Don't try anything during the first two rounds. Just observe. I wish I were out there with you. Bring back as much information as you can. Let's talk between charges. It's always the last three rounds that count."

"I will be a good boy," Balto rumbled calmly. Jan admired his placidity at a time like this.

Jan ran and brought a pan with shima powder. "Here," he said. "Work this into your hands so that they won't sweat. Then you had better mount."

Balto powdered, rubbed and slapped his hands. Then he led the way into the outer courtyard. Fleatcher waited in the center of the crowded, busy space—a

magnificent, blue-furred, six-legged, red-eyes, triple-
humped wonder topped by a gorgeous white saddle
between its second and third humps. Two stableboys
rubbed Fleatcher's humps to stimulate the hormone
glands; they sneezed repeatedly as the acrid chemical
mixed with Fleatcher's blood. Balto saw Poruscht as
well, all saddled and ready just in case. Carefully
watched by Fangano guards, chemists from the Contortus camp checked the gleaming heads of lances to
the left; they swabbed the metal with cotton strips
dunked into small phials of chemicals they carried in
belts around their waist.

Balto mounted and looked down at Jan.

Jan slapped his exposed knee. "May this be your
day, my lord," he said.

Then the trumpets sounded, and Balto urged Fleatcher out through an opening, out through the Fangano
perimeter fence, into the arena. His people surged out
after him, Jan at their head.

The organizers of the games had arranged Tent City
in a huge circle around an open space. Mount Crasnus
looked down upon the scene from the north; it blocked
the view of Dominus, which hovered off Simalta on the
other side. Hundreds of tents, a dozen shapes—peaked,
domed, air-supported, square-rigged, onion-form.
Bright colors. Hundreds of family pennants flew and
cracked in the brisk westerly wind, the first sign of the
tumultuous stormy season which would succeed the
balmy halfyear.

People. They sat on the edge of the gigantic circle, a
belt of faces and bodies, the color of a crazy-quilt.
Balto admired Mart's organizational abilities. Cush
had turned out quite a crowd.

Directly opposite Balto was the Contortus complex,

a red canvas fortress composed of peak-style tents; each of the fourteen peaks carried the red banner with the yellow figure of the leaping felina.

Balto gazed across the vast expanse of the jousting field seeking his enemy—and then he saw Ignazio emerge, mounted on Glitsch. The distance was too great to see much more than rider and mount. Balto listened to the roaring of the crowd for a second, collecting himself one final time; then he turned to his right, toward the roofed-over stands where the lords and ladies sat—a bright, distant shimmering of gold, white, blue, and silver robes. He made for the subdivided section in the center of the stands. The Concession senators sat there, waiting for the contestants.

Fleatcher rocked, bounched, and bobbled him. With sideways glances Balto observed Ignazio's approach and so timed his movement toward the stands that both of them arrived before the Senate at the same time.

"I'm Balto Fangano, head of my family," Balto called up, addressing Fantidaimi. "Under the provisions of Basic Concession Law, Rubric 18, as amended, I challenge Ignazio Contortus to a blood joust. The challenge is not personal. My objective is to acquire the position of Controller Tundrati now held by Ignazio."

The senators wore grave expressions. All were older men, family members of the "original eleven," the founders of the Fillippi Investment Combine which had later become the Fillippi Concession.

Fantidaimi turned to Ignazio. The senator had a very big forehead and thin, grey hair which fell back on his skull like beach-grass under an off-shore breeze.

"Do you accept the challenge, Ignazio, or do you yield your post without contest."

"I accept the challenge," Ignazio said. "I would

remind the lords that Rubric 18, as amended, requires that I be killed in battle before any succession is implemented."

Balto observed his oponent. The face was even more pudgy than he remembered; the eyes were nearly hidden behind hillocks of fat.

"We are aware of the language of the law," Fantidaimi said. He spoke downwards. The lords were high on their platform, the jousters below them on the turf. "To be precise, however," Fantidaimi added, "to meet this challenge you must ride five voltas. If you survive all five, you remain Controller of Tundrati. But if you refuse to show, you lose your post."

Ignazio nodded. "That's understood. I meant to point out to the lords that tafpa jousts are seldom fatal. The Lord Fangano has chosen a contest ill-suited to serve his stated purpose. Perhaps the lord would consider a more definitive challenge?"

"The choice is up to Lord Fangano," the senator said. "Rubric seventeen gives the challenger choice of weapons. I believe your family insisted on that clause when the amendments were voted."

"I'm quite satisfied," Balto rumbled.

"In that case, barring objections, the Senate grants the joust." He looked at his colleagues for confirmation. The others made no move. "Very well. Lords you may proceed. You have five rounds."

The jousters turned their tafpas, Balto to the right, Ignazio to the left; then they began the slow trot around the periphery of the circle.

Halfway around the field, Fleatcher shuddered and threw himself into the volta. As always, Balto found the experience exhilarating. They flew. The people on the ground became a blurr. He only heard their lusty cheering as he passed. They waved hats and scarves.

He saw Ignazio moving in the opposite direction. He rode past the Contortus tents and once again past the stands. Arriving again at his own complex, he made a quick, deft pace change and re-entered the sheltering canvas walls of his compound.

Jan already waited, holding the lance.

Balto took the heavy weapon and stuck its butt into a leather pocket under his right arm; then he raised the glinting tip into the vertical. The trumpets sounded again.

"Remember, my lord, go easy."

Balto nodded and gave rein to Fleatcher. The beast burned under hormone stimulation and shot forward like an arrow. Jan and the others in the compound surged out in Fleatcher's wake to take up positions outside the complex once again.

Jan watched the engagement through a pair of binoculars. The jousters raced around the circle twice in opposite directions as the crowd took up the traditional chant: "Hit, hit, hit, hit." The tafpas churned at breathless speed, legs almost invisible. They reached the orange turning stakes sunk into the turf at either end of the field. Signalled by their riders, the animals twisted toward the center of the circle, and then the jousters hurled themselves toward each other at fantastic speeds. Their lances clashed briefly; lance tips flashed in the sun. Then the riders were separated; each turned toward his compound. The first round was over.

The crowd expressed its disappointment in a series of loud hoots.

Jan shook his head. He couldn't understand it. Ignazio had ridden Glitsch in an impossibly hapless manner. Brudd could have done a better job. *Fillip,* for God's sake, could have whipped Ignazio, in this sorry engagement. Could this be a ruse? One down, four to go. I'll have to see the second round, Jan thought.

Balto burst into the group, restraining Fleatcher. His big, wide face was sweaty and red.

"I could have finished that clown in the first round," he shouted. He lowered his lance; attendants checked it for cracks and general soundness. "I'm going out there and spear him right through his heart. He can't even ride!"

"You will *not*," Jan cried. "You will do no such thing, my lord. It's an old trick of the trade. You're *supposed* to feel over-confident."

"You're wrong, Jan. This clown can't even ride."

"He rode well enough in the exhibition round," Jan said, recalling Ignazio as he had sped past, his long, bleached hair flying in the air. "I watched him. I assure you, this has to be a ruse. Crowd him a little. Aim for an arm. But don't get too close. And for God's sake be careful."

"I'll spear him for you, Jan."

"Dammit, my lord, please do as I tell you."

"Glitsch shied, just like you said he would. It would've been easy."

The trumpet sounded.

"Please do as I tell you, lord."

Jan watched anxiously, hoping that the lord would be obedient, and soon noted that Balto had grown bolder. He drove Fleatcher straight at Glitsch—but aimed at an arm, thank God for that! The animals collided, the lances cracked, "*Good* show," Jan cried. Balto had been magnificient.

As the combatants separated, Jan followed Ignazio's return to the Contortus complex through his binoculars. Ignazio's left arm hung limp; it dangled and wobbled like something dead—severed tendons, slashed muscles . . . "*Good* show," Jan murmured, very pleased with the round.

Balto roared to a halt, flushed, angry, and triumphant. Blood flecked the vicious tip of his lance.

"Damn you cautious Cush types," he yelled, oblivious of the fact that strangers might hear him. "I could've had him. I had a shot at his neck, right here." He pointed to his own trunk-like neck. "I practically tore his arm off."

"He is yours, my lord," Jan said and smiled. "But be cautious." He hit Fleatcher on the rump as the trumpet sounded again.

Two down, three to go.

Ignazio came riding out and made his circle with his left arm limp. He passed the Fangano tents at great speed, but Jan clearly saw the dead arm tied to the saddle. Unbalanced and swaying, he moved toward Balto exposed like a straw dummy, his lance low and nearly plowing turf. Balto had no difficulties. He drove his lance right into Ignazio's groin; Ignazio nearly came off his mount; his twisting body snapped Balto's lance at the tip. Then Glitsch turned and carried the man away. Ignazio hung down on one side, appearing to be tied to Glitsch; he trailed a stream of blood.

It's all over, Jan thought. The crowd thought so too. The lords and ladies in the stands were clearly of the same mind. A great roar rose toward the sky and echoed back from Mount Crasnus.

Balto returned, smiling. "Give me a new lance," he cried, throwing his broken stump to the ground. "Not that I'll need one. He won't come out again. The tip is in his guts. He is finished. Looks like we've won, my friend."

"Fompus," cried an excited voice through the tent flap. "Fompus Leo! Come quickly. We have radio."

Leo had joined the watchers. "Not now," he called with rare impatience.

The trumpet sounded. Balto turned Fleatcher and faced the far-away Contortus tents again. He had to hold the beast in check. Fleatcher longed to run; he steamed with heat, sweat, and lather, and the pungent reek of hormone rose with the steam from his humps. Balto, Jan, Leo, the surging crowd—all expected to see a servant with the white pennant that signified "I'll concede defeat."

The crowd waited. The time was drawing out.

"Fompus, hurry. It's Fillip. He has the girl."

But no one heard the voice. The crowd caught its breath in shock and surprise. Instead of the servant with the white pennant, Ignazio appeared again opposite the field.

"Damn," shouted Balto and released Fleatcher. He shot forward. There was no time for conversation.

"Damnation, Zullus, I don't care *what's* going on. Get him! *Drag* him to the radio if you have to."

Rage and frustration twisted Fillip's otherwise so fat and placid features. "Bumbling idiots," he cried, speaking to a girl who wore a tundratus uniform. Black hair streaked blond in the center covered her head. "They are in the middle of the joust," he said. "Balto has to know that he is fighting surrogates. Those slaves are probably twice as good as Ignazio."

Fillip faced a radio console; Sophie squatted next to him. Three Contortus palace guards lay on the floor nearby; they slept despite their shackles and their gags. Smashed radio equipment and other debris littered the room.

Fillip had worked for hours to build a radio from all this wreakage. He had vital intelligence to give. And that stupid Zullus down below couldn't get Leo's attention!

"Damn," he said. "Come on, Leo. Get a move on."

Sophie shared his anxiety. Both stared at the radio.

The reek of burning and of spent explosives thickened the atmosphere despite a movement of air through the palace. A strong westerly blew outdoors carrying bits of paper down the wide, empty reaches of the Circumferential beyond the broken windows.

Fillip made a note to douse that smoldering fire as soon as he had gotten through. The credenza burned back there. The couch still smoldered.

The Contorti had tried everything, but he had survived and conquered.

The night seemed like a nightmare now—a burning, ear-shattering, flashing dream. He had fought himself as much as he had fought these three. They were just Menoma-soldiers after all, and he had known that they would exhaust their beam-guns sooner or later. But sleep had almost won the battle. You can't sleep; you can't relax the pressure. Drive those *dubu-dam-dam* bullets through the wooden table. Keep them squirming. Make them use those beamers.

It had been his second sleepless night. What terror when he had awakened after eye-wink-long naps! Drive those bullets.

During the night he had become aware once more of the dull, heavy thumping from below. The thumping came in answer to his shots, and he realized that palace people were locked up in the cellar. They signalled and called him.

In the end he had won the battle against himself, against these men. The Contortus guns had failed at early light. He had heard the characteristic "slurrp" sound of empty beamers. When he had heard the sound five times, he had risen from behind the credenza, no longer opposed.

Now he crouched over his home-made radio in a fury of frustration. "Where *is* that man," he hissed.

As if in answer he heard Leo's voice, a little distorted. The set was barely functioning.

"Fompus? Fillip here. Listen to me carefully. Balto is fighting surrogates. They are Menoma-slaves made to look like Ignazio. They have at least five slaves down there and maybe more."

"Are you sure of this?" The crackling transmission carried only the words, not the intonation.

"As sure as any man can be," Fillip said.

"The girl?"

"Yes. Sophie found the surrogates. In a plastic surgery ward."

"Are you safe?"

"*Now* we are," Fillip answered. He glanced sideways at the sleeping soldiers and at trusty *dubu-dam-dam* by his side.

"Stand by. I'll be back. Good work."

The channel fell silent.

Fillip turned to Sophie. "See?" he said, beaming. "Simple. Nothing much to it. Five or six words, and the message is down there. Good work, folks. See you later."

They both laughed. For the first time in many hours, they could relax.

Jan watched the fourth round in utter disbelief. The antagonists circled the field again, and Jan inspected Ignazio as he flashed by at Glitsch's incredible speed. He sensed some sort of commotion behind him; someone dragged Leo away, protesting, but Jan paid no attention. His mind was on Ignazio. The left arm no longer dangled. It had been restored miraculously; Ignazio used it freely to urge Glitsch forward and to keep his balance at volta speed. But now a large, conspicuous, blood-stained bandage covered Ignazio's center. Glitsch seemed in good shape and churned around the circle lustily tossing torn turf into the air.

Jan refused to believe it. They had to be using a drug, a drug, a drug. His thoughts grew hysterical. No one could ride a tafpa with a lance-tip in his innards. The lance head was twelve centimeters long, six centimeters wide, three centimeters thick and had a rough, sharp, double-edged blade and two vicious barbs. With that in his bowels, a man could not survive—much less ride the volta. And in the three minutes allowed between rounds, even the fastest surgeon couldn't operate.

A drug, he thought. Penta is right. This isn't natural.

The beasts headed in, toward the center.

Jan noted that Fompus Leo had returned and now stood next to him again.

Balto took the initiative once more and made for Ignazio on a collision course. Sparks flew as the lance-heads struck. And again Balto prevailed. The churn of tafpas, bodies, and lances obscured this view, but Jan judged that Balto's lance entered Ignazio's shoulder between arm-guards and breast plates—on the right side this time.

Balto looked both angry and puzzled. He threw down his broken stump with a disgusted expression.

Leo stepped forward. "Listen to me, Balto, Jan." The urgency of his voice caused Balto to lean down in response. "We've just received intelligence from Castle. It explains everything. The Contorti are using surrogates against us—conditioned slaves with Ignazio's face."

Balto shook his head. He didn't seem to understand.

"Plastic surgery," Leo said. "That's why Ignazio always survives his duels. He never fights them. Someone else dies for him."

Comprehension dawned on Balto's and Jan's faces.

"Now pay attention to me. I have a plan. I think it will ensure our victory after all. But you must knock him off his tafpa and stick a lance right through him— and in such a way that everyone can see it. I can't explain more now," the fompus concluded. "Just do it. Then ride up to the Senate and claim victory."

The trumpet sounded.

"Go in as before," Jan shouted. "Do a pace-change to the side at the last second. Try to take him from the side this time."

Jan hoped Balto had heard the words as he roared off.

Jan watched the jousters circle for nearly an entire round before the realization hit him. Intelligence from Castle!

"Leo!" he cried. "Leo?"

The fompus put a soothing hand on his shoulder. "She's safe and sound," he said.

Jan watched this last and final volta awash in emotions he could no longer master. Sophie was safe—and his heart exulted with joy. But the surrogates on the field filled him with dread. Could Balto still joust? Some person who looked like Ignazio Contortus had emerged to fight a fifth engagement, and that sufficed to satisfy the conditions of the challenge. Even if Balto killed the surrogate, the real Ignazio was still alive; Drusilla would produce him later and claim a draw. And that would mean defeat for Cush.

What did Leo have in mind? What was his plan?

There would be time to look into that later. Now Jan witnessed the last collision. The crowd had come to its feet during the final rush of tafpas around the circle. A death-like stillness lay over the field. No one shouted "Hit, hit, hit." Only the pennants cracked and fluttered in the wind, and the thud of hoofs pounding the turf reverberated dully underfoot.

Balto had heard Jan. At the last second, he executed that incredible change of pace which only a tafpa could accomplish at that speed—a leap into the air and a sharp twist of the trunk. Fleatcher landed at right angles from Glitsch, his six legs churning. Balto's lance transfixed the surrogate, and Fleatcher crashed into Glitsch from behind. Men and mounts tumbled to the ground.

Pesudo-Ignazio fell forward. Balto's lance had entered his back and had passed right through him. The lance tip sank into the turf as he fell. The surrogate, on hands and knees, strained to rise. Jan could see him half succeeding, but the effort was too great. Blood gushed from the creature's mouth and wound and ran down in volume, discoloring the shaft of the lance. The slave suddenly shuddered and fell forward.

The tafpa had scrambled up again. Balto walked over to his antagonist and with a foot nudged him over onto his side, thus revealing the crimson lance tip again. He bent down and swept aside the bleached hair that had fallen over the surrogate's face. For a very long moment he regarded the face. Then he walked back to Fleatcher and lept into the saddle. As he loped off toward the covered stands where the Senate sat, a race developed between the crowd and a wedge-shaped formation of Contortus guards. All made for the center. The guards must have been prepared for this. They ran quickly and in tight formation, beam-guns extended at the ready. They reached the body first and surrounded it. Then slowly, as a body, they moved off toward the tents of the leaping felina.

Balto stopped Fleatcher in front of the Senate and wiped his face with a hand.

"I hereby claim victory under Rubric Ninteen of Concession Law," he rumbled, addressing Fantidaimi. "I have killed him before your very eyes. You saw him die. I demand that you set a swearing time. Under Rubric Twenty, the Senate may waive the four-day rule. Under the circumstances, I believe a waiver is appropriate, and I respectfully request it."

He felt the pressure of people behind him. They jostled and moved;

"You have been valiant, Balto Fangano," Fantidaimi said. He looked at the other senators. All of them continued to look grave. "Any objections to a waiver?" The men were silent. "In that case the time will be set for tomorrow, at high noon, in this place."

A cheer went up from the crowd. Balto felt hands reaching for him. He was lifted from the tafpa and hoisted high above the crowd.

They started to yell, "Fangano, Fangano," but the three syllables were too awkward to yell. So they switched to, "Balto, Bal-to, Bal-to," and carried him toward his tents.

From this raised vantage point, Balto could see that the Contortus complex was surrounded by a wall of palace guards standing shoulder to shoulder, beam-guns extended, as if anticipating an attack. Amidst the sea of happy and smiling faces, his was the only somber expression.

19 — THE ADVENT OF SOLUMNOS TECK

After the joust we must assemble again for a retros-
pective review . . . It may be instructive, after the
event, to see how my strategy worked out.
                              —*Farnit Drusilla, Chief Fompus of*
                              the Contorti

Just within the Contortus complex, inside the
canvas-shielded area, Drusilla inspected the human
wreckage. The friends lay in pools of blood, their
bodies torn and mangled by Balto Fangano's lance.
Slaves poured acid over the dead faces, and the hiss-
ing, steaming liquid gave off a pungent smell.
Glitsch stood to one side, reeking and steaming, but
no one paid any attention to the beast.

On first assessment, Drusilla decided, he was neither
pleased nor displeased with the outcome. The joust
could have gone better, but it could also have gone
worse. True, the last engagement had been a sour note.
He recalled how the friend had looked with a lance
stuck through his body and how the friend had shuddered before giving up the ghost. Fangano had left a
dead man out there, but the Senate would uphold the
Contorti when they saw Ignazio alive. The Senate was
weak and Drusilla's will adamant. He would prevail.

The drift of his own thoughts alarmed the fompus suddenly. He dismissed that line of argument. It arose from fear and wishful thinking. He had witnessed a defeat out there, a rout. The Contorti had staged a disaster. Still, not everything was lost. He still had force, he had the tundrati, and if all else failed he had a scout only he knew about. He would ripple his muscles in front of the Senate, and when they were properly frightened, he would show them Ignazio and give them a face-saving way out of the dilemma. Better to close an eye over the Contortus fraud then have tundrati attack.

Teck would be pleased by this turn of events. He would try to exploit the situation—and Drusilla was prepared to eat his own words to some extent. But he had done that before and would survive.

Then, for the second time today, Drusilla experienced doubt. Maybe I won't survive, he thought.

Events had taken a curiously fatal direction recently and everything had gone awry. He had rescued Brudd only to discover that the man knew nothing. Brudd lay in chains, awaiting punishment—but that was nothing to cheer about. He had just learned that an agent had escaped from the Contortus palace. She had seen the surrogates still left up there. She might be in touch with the Fanganos or the Senate, and the secret of Ignazio's fabulous luck would remain a secret no more. Drusilla had one course of action left. Could that, too, go wrong? No. He was sure about one thing. No one could stand up to three thousand Gash tundrati, and a military takeover would certainly succeed. Then, suddenly, Drusilla began to smile. If it came to that, he thought, if the rotten fabric of constitutional government would be sundered once and for all anyway, he had no need of the Contortus family. He could rule in his own name. The Contorti must go! They must go first.

Still smiling, his eyes to the ground in concentration, he began to formulate a plan. Just then a hand tugged his sleeve and a boy handed him a folded message.

Drusilla unfolded the note. "Dear Farnit," he read. "Could you join me quickly in my tent? A minor matter has come up."

Drusilla looked about. During the last minute or so, tundrati from Gash had quietly filed into the courtyard. Their commander stood near the exit that led to the tents, and his face revealed his orders.

Drusilla looked down on the note again. The handwriting and the signature were Ignazio's. The coy tone and the unstated, deadly intent of the words had been supplied by Teck. Icy claws of foreboding gripped Drusilla's innards. He turned toward the tents, and as he did the tundrati turned with him.

Solumnos Teck stood at the head of a large table. The family members sat around the table forming a horseshoe; Teck's own staff occupied chairs behind them. Drusilla had just been led away. Teck cleared his throat.

"Now that we have dealt with Farnit," he said, "let's go to work."

Through sparkling, rimless glasses he surveyed the assembly with inward satisfaction. He had anticipated this pleasure ever since news of the Faltara joust had come to him some weeks ago. He had seized his opportunity, and he had been victorious. Now for the first time he tasted the power that had been Drusilla's, and he found it even more pleasing in actuality than it had been in anticipation.

"If you would prefer, lady and lords," he said, "my staff and I could withdraw. On the other hand . . ."

"We will stay, Sol," said the Deep One, Lord Cullu. "We need to be informed."

The other members of the family nodded. All were here, all of Teck's supporters: Thamo, Fenid, Exume, and Glamos—long-faced men who resembled Cullu—and blowsy, matronly Csicsa, who took after Ignazio. Ignazio himself appeared relaxed and at ease in the lap of his family. He hadn't raised a single finger to defend his fompus. He appeared, in fact, glad to see the bald monster humbled. In *his* lap was a felina kitten, a playful yellow ball; attracted by the glitter of diamonds on his shoulder, it tried to crawl up Ignazio's tunic.

"By all means stay," Teck said. "I wouldn't have it otherwise."

"We trust you entirely, dear boy," over-ripe Csicsa cried, a little too loudly, as was her way. In disregard of Castle decorum she wore a red robe splashed with large yellow circles. "It's so much fun, this . . . this power politics."

Teck couldn't agree with her more. "My lady," he said, "I will work diligently to deserve your trust." The ingratiating tone was a tool of power, and he used it skillfully and gladly. In no time at all they would get bored with participation, and then he would have free rein. And power politics *was* wonderfully entertaining.

Teck turned a somewhat colder eye toward his staff. He nodded to the Colonel of the Palace Guard. "The numbers, if you please, Rhumus." Colonel Rhumus had replaced Lupus a few minutes ago. Lupus was of the old guard, and he had had to go.

The colonel rose quickly and stepped to some boards arranged on an easel. He removed a blank board used as a cover and revealed a chart. At the same time, he pushed a button on a device the size of a pen, and it grew into a slender, silvery pointer.

The head of a guard captain appeared through the tent flap. "Fompus," he said, "pardon the intrusion, but you didn't give instructions on how . . ." The captain seemed embarrassed.

"Ah, yes," Teck said. He mused for a second. "By strangulation," he said. (That would please the family.)

As the guard's head vanished, Teck sat down and nodded to his new colonel. The pointer moved smartly to a column of figures on the left side of the chart.

"First, our side," the colonel said. "We have the palace guard, eighty men." The pointer skipped. "The Castle reserve, two hundred." It skipped again. "Thirty-five hundred men on Gash, the planetary reserve. Another five hundred more from Gash are already on Faltara, as you know, to secure the island during the siege. Finally—" the pointer skipped "—we have five hundred new tundrati recruits on eight flower islands, but they must be assembled and flown in." He looked up.

"That's nearly forty-three hundred men," Teck said. "What about the enemy?"

The pointer moved smartly to the right.

"At last count the total manpower of palace guards—all families not counting our own—was twelve hundred men. At least nine hundred are on Dominus to guard family properties. The rest are down here."

"So the other side has three hundred effectives."

"Yes, chief fompus—provided we succeed in blocking those that are still on Dominus."

"Very well," Teck said. "We have overwhelming superiority in numbers. And the timing?"

The colonel nodded.

"It's four o'clock. The Gash tundrati presently on Faltara are concentrated in this area." He had moved over and now pointed to the site of the fair grounds on a large map of Faltara. "They are no problem." He turned back to Teck. "The Castle reserve up on Dominus—we could get all of them down here by midnight using one aircraft. The people on Gash could get here by morning using their own hydrofoils. The problem is assembling the five hundred new recruits from the other islands. We have severe fuel limitations."

"Your best guess, Colonel?" Teck was pleased by his own tone. He had brought off the crisp, military style and knew that the family watched with admiration. Only Cullu stared without expression—as he always did.

"The five hundred could be here by midnight or early in the morning at the latest."

"Excellent, excellent. We must be in place by high noon. Anything else?"

"Yes, chief fompus. The new recruits must be delivered to Riondi the day after tomorrow. So we can't use them for a protracted engagement."

Teck smiled and looked at the family. "I don't expect an engagement, protracted or otherwise. As you know, Rhumus, this is merely a show of force." He mused for a second; all eyes were on him. "And if there is an engagement, it'll be short and sweet."

He rose to his feet. "Let's get to work," he said, repeating his opening statement. "Colonel, I give you charge of the Faltara side of the operation. I want you to notify the occupation commander. Get the Castle reserve down here. And coordinate all movements."

He turned to Huroka. "You will ensure that the new

recruits are delivered. I want you to call every Tower director. Personally. Sicofanta here will help you with logistics. I will personally handle the shock troops of Gash. I see them as our main striking force, of course. I want running reports from everyone. I will make all the decisions. That's all."

He turned to the family for some amiable chit-chat—and to explain what all this meant in terms even autumnal Csicsa could understand. After a while he excused himself to organize a "war room" as he called it.

20 — A NIGHT OF MOTION

*Never imagine, not even for a moment, that you are
the revolution. The revolution is the people. Learn to
be humble. If you put on airs, you won't be able to
resist the vortex of power when we're victorious.*
> —Penta Mart, Twentieth
> Commencement Address

Colonel Tussalla Robartus stood behind a desk in the
headquarters building of the Island of Gash. Some
minutes earlier, the desk had belonged to General
Mondo, commander of the military island. General
Mondo's papers, general Mondo's snuff box, General Mondo's mustache brush, General Mondo's lac tea
cup (half full) still stood on the desk. General Mondo's
ancestors hung framed on the walls. The general himself lay on the carpet next to the desk.

Robartus drew closer to the active visiphone on General Mondo's desk; he leaned into it so that the caller on
the other end could only see Robartus' square-jawed
face, blue eyes under sandy lashes, and the hooked scar
on the colonel's face.

Robartus' caller had severely parted hair—so flat, so
slick, so black that it looked like paint. The man trembled with fury but tried to control himself. He was
Solumnos Teck, as Robartus knew—not only because

Teck had announced himself (and had emphasized pointedly that he was now Chief Fompus), but because Robartus had talked to Penta Mart on the transporter's radio. Mart had said that Drusilla had been deposed. Mart roamed about somewhere on Faltara, making like a native, but he had his finger in the battle anyway.

Robartus noted that Sol Teck sat in some sort of command post the Contorti were setting up. He saw parts of technicians stringing wire; messages were pushed in front of Teck by hands that came in and out of the screen. Radio traffic crackled and voices buzzed around the fompus.

Robartus had arrived just in the nick of time. Out in the hall he could still hear commotion. General Mondo groaned by his feet with a gag in his mouth. The bushy grey moustaches half covered the fat strip of black insulation that held a wad of paper in place.

"I'm sorry to upset you, fompus," Robartus said, "but facts are facts. I was assigned as Deputy Commander of Gash three weeks ago. And believe me, fompus, General Mondo doesn't ask *me* for permission to go on leave. He wanted to see the joust, I understand. He is down there somewhere. He is nearer to you than he is to me."

Mondo groaned under the desk. Robartus kicked him—hard.

"I am in command here—and entirely at your service."

Down on the Island of Faltara, Teck stared into his visiscreen and studied this sandy-haired soldier with some distaste. The man's tunic was open at the neck and showed a hairy chest. The soldier seemed to have a red spot on his forehead as if he had been in some sort of scuffle. The fompus felt unsure. Now he regretted the summary execution of Drusilla's key aides. He didn't remember the transfer of this man. He could ask for a record check, but in the mad-house he was in now, that seemed impractical.

"You say you were on Riondi?" he asked uncertainly.

"Yes, sir. Commanding Officer, One-oh-eighth Radar Track Battalion." Robartus wished his men wouldn't make such a racket. They seemed to enjoy roughing up the fompa inside the headquarters.

"All right, Robartus—that *is* your name? Very well, Robartus, I will give you some orders that I want carried out promptly."

"Yes, sir."

"I want you to move your entire force to Faltara by hydrofoil. We have no aircraft to spare. I want them here early in the morning. You will land on West Shore, South Bosom, and march to the fair grounds, ready for combat."

In the background Robartus heard a file cabinet crash to the floor.

"We will be there, fompus. You can rely on Gash." He paused and seemed to swallow with a big bobbling of his Adam's apple. "Provided, of course, that we can get the hydrofoils running."

Robartus threw a glance through the window on his right. Three giant hydrofoils lay anchored off one end of a bleak, barren arm of the island. Between the headquarters building and the ships stood wooden barracks, two rows face to face. In the middle of that dull avenue the leaping felina banner flapped on top of a tall pole.

"What do you mean, when you get the hydrofoils running?"

Teck's composure had begun to crack, Robartus noted. The rimless glasses were fogging up.

"Well, sir," he said, "the fact is that we can't move without our hydrofoils—unless you want to send us those choppers you say you haven't got."

"I told you that choppers are out," Teck cried. "What's wrong with the hydrofoils?" Teck had a feeling that this Robartus was either teasing him or stupid. Gash without transport—that seemed unreal, somehow.

"A little of this, a little of that, fompus," Robartus said. "Take the case of one-oh-four. Now we had the engine out for maintenance on that old swan, and the hoist pallet developed a levitron leak while the men were eating—"

"Listen here, Robartus. I don't want to hear about your petty troubles. Do you mean to tell me that you have *no* transport?"

Robartus scratched his scar and screwed up his face in a gesture meant to convey embarrassment. "Well, sir, there's one-oh-six. She *limps* along, you know, at half speed. But she will only hold eight hundred men." Then he appeared to get an idea. His eyes opened wide. "Hey, fompus, I just had an idea. If you could send the old swan on Faltara—"

"There isn't time for that. You say you have one operational hydrofoil?

"One-oh-six, sir. She limps along. A twisted air-van slows her down to half speed."

"Can you fix it?"

"Certainly, we can. I have been trying to tell you." He kicked Mondo again; the general's moans were growing loud enough so that Teck might hear them. "We are working on all of them. One-oh-three, her rudder mechanism went screwy, when—"

"Spare me that, Robartus. I will send our own hydro to you. You get those ships fixed and meet it half way."

"We are working hard, fompus. We will be there; it's just likely to be a little slow."

Teck screwed up his face and leaned into the vis-iphone screen. He pointed a finger at Robartus. The finger grew abnormally large as it came nearer. It wagged with emphasis.

"You had better *move*, Robartus. I am holding you personally responsible. If you fail me on this, you're through. Understand? Through."

"Yes sir. But I am only human." Robartus tried to sound afraid. "If one-oh-four's engine block is cracked—"

But Teck had already cut the connection. Robartus expelled air. Then he broke into a hearty laugh. He kicked Mondo again, playfully this time.

"How did you like that, general?" he asked. "How was that for an impromptu performance?"

"You were absolutely right," came Fillip's voice over the radio. "The Contorti are gathering every tundratus they can find up here. The men have a deep command to gather at the airport, and to the best of our ability to determine, they are being moved down to the island in batches in a single chopper."

"What sort of tundrati?" Jan asked. He sat in the brightly lit Fangano communications tent; night had set in, but the tent was a hive of activity. Runners came in and out and gave their messages to Leo and Balto who stood before a large map of Faltara.

"Castle security forces," Fillip said. "Palace guards from all sorts of families are trying to get down too, but they can't get to the airport; the Contorti have the approaches blocked. So all these people are milling about on the street. It's a mess up here. What about you people?"

"Everything is running smoothly in our shop," Jan said, "but outside there is panic. Rumors are flying; the families are frantic and trying to organize—without much success. We hear that Drusilla has been strangled and that Sol Teck has taken charge. He is sending soldiers all over the place. Thousands of people came for the joust, and they are still out there camping out and cooking on huge fires. Teck chases them away from time to time, but they come drifting back the moment the tundrati leave. And more people are coming all the time. The roads are supposed to be clogged by masses of people."

"Imagine that," Fillip said. "I wonder who told them to come?"

"Who indeed?" Jan said smiling.

"The message I sent you earlier—did you people make good use of it?"

"Very good use," Jan said. "Without that little message of yours, we might have lost the joust. You weren't here to see the show, but you made it the good show it was."

"Is there anything you want me to do?"

"Yes," Jan said. "Two things. Check on the airport situation and get back to us again. And let me speak to Sophie."

"I wondered when you would come around to that," Fillip said. "Here she is."

Teck wondered how many hours he had spent behind this command post desk. Six? Seven? Eight? Eight gruelling hours of work, he guessed—and yet the messages were coming faster than ever. Almost every other minute another sweaty guard or clerk ran in with news. The radio operator seated near him spoke incessantly to roving units and turned to him for guidance. Faces waited for him on three visiphones. And Lord Cullu pestered him for news at regular intervals. Draped in the cool folds of a golden robe, the Deep One reclined to the left in a translucent inflatochair, and his steady, observing gaze distracted Teck and made him nervous. He wished that the Deep One would get off that chair and go to bed.

Teck felt himself submerged in a roaring sea of information, and as he turned to yet another visiphone caller, a fleeting thought of Drusilla crossed his mind. He recalled the sight of the dead fompus, his neck twisted, the copper-colored skull now pale—like a lamp whose light had been extinguished. Dead eyes had stared at Teck, and with a shudder he had told a slave to shut them. Even in death those eyes had had a pointed and commanding quality. He wondered how Drusilla would have managed this tidal wave of information, but then he suppressed the thought that Drusilla's eyes might have commanded these waves to be still.

"Robartus, dammit, man, are you still back there?" He knew he must stay cool, like Drusilla would have been—no, that was the wrong comparison.

"We've got one-oh-six working, fompus," Robartus said. "She's limping out to sea now."

"It's midnight, man. You must do better than that."

"We are just plain unlucky, fompus. When we stripped the gears on one-oh-four—"

"Get *on* with it, Robartus. Get out there and *work*."

Teck shut off that tauntingly exasperating face. Damn that man. Then he turned in response to the radio operator's call.

"What is it, Mastu?"

"Eight more reports have come in, sir," the operator said. "That mob from Simalta has reached the Crasnus approaches. They have split into three columns and they are coming up toward the passes."

"Get me Colonel Rhumus on the line."

"He *is* on the line, sir." Mastu pointed at one of the visiscreens.

Yes, Rhumus waited. Another visiphone buzzed. Teck clicked it on and the grey screen resolved into the pinched, wrinkled features of Huroka. "Hold the line, Huroka. I will be with you in a second."

For a minute now a dark shape had hovered in front of Teck's desk. He had sent this clerk out on an errand about an hour ago, but now he could not recall what he had told the man to do.

"Sit *down*, will you," he snapped at the clerk, his self-control shaken. "Can't you see that I am busy?" Then, with renewed effort, icily: "I'll be with you in a minute."

He turned to the new Colonel of the Palace Guard and switched on the audio channel. Behind Rhumus he could see the inside of Dominus' airport where the colonel had established a command post of his own. Teck saw masses of tundrati lounging in clumps.

"Listen, Rhumus," he said. "I want you to send parties out to block the Crasnus passes on our side. I don't want any mobs down here. I have enough to do. They are streaming up from the south, too. Have you sent somebody to stop them?"

"They left an hour ago."

"Well, that's encouraging."

All those people streaming toward the Fairgrounds of Faltara worried Teck no end. The joust was over and yet they were still coming in large masses and from all directions. Why? He made a mental note to think about that—as soon as he found a minute's time to spare.

"I also have some bad news," Rhumus said.

Teck stared. How much of this conversation could the Deep One hear? Cullu looked as if he slept, but then he always looked like that. Teck reached forward and turned the audio.

"What is it this time?" he asked, half whispering.

"Our transport chopper is down, and we still have eighty men up here."

Teck resented it. All this could not be happening to him. He had had an entirely different concept of command. He had seen Drusilla do it. Drusilla had given orders, and everyone had obeyed. Hydrofoils didn't limp, chopters didn't fail. Mysterious crowds didn't materialize. Everything went smoothly. He realized he didn't *like* to be here. He didn't want all these people telling him why they couldn't do things.

"Why?" he said. "Why is that goddamned chopper down?"

"Somebody shot through the levitron tank, shot it all full of holes."

"That's impossible. The tanks are lead-shielded."

"Fompus, I *know* that," the colonel said, with a hint of irritation. "Whoever did it didn't use a beamer. He used some sort of projectile weapon. Explosive bullets. Made a hellish racket. He also killed two pilots."

"Did you get him?"

"No, fompus, we didn't. There are several hundred palace guards milling around out there. It's dark. It's confusing."

"Are you repairing the ship?"

"As best we can. It's a longish job. It will take hours."

"Well, send those blocking parties to the passes."

"Will do, fompus."

"I'll be with you in a minute, Huroka," Teck said, switching the little man on and then off. He gestured to the clerk who was still waiting, and the clerk came near. Two more messengers arrived and took up positions some distance from the desk in front of some large maps. Staff officers were posting tundrati dispositions on those maps. A glance told Teck that his forces were widely scattered. Those damned mobs. Mastu slipped him a written message. He glanced at it with distaste.

FALTARA HYDROFOIL WELL PAST MID-POINT. NO SIGN OF GASH SHIPS. GASH DOES NOT RESPOND TO RADIO. REQUEST INSTRUCTIONS.

Three thousand men. Where were those three thousand men. He could use them now for crowd control. He bent down to his radio operator. "Tell them to go on toward Gash," he said and then turned to the clerk. "Well?"

"The lords have broken off the meeting."

Teck remembered now where he had sent this man. Fantidaimi had called a meeting of the lords. Contorti had not been invited. This clerk brought him intelligence about the meeting.

"And?"

"They tried to organize themselves and to select a commander. They voted for Balto Fangano, but Lord Balto refused."

"Refused?"

"Yes. He said he would have no part of an armed insurrection against the Contorti. He said the law would uphold him. He relied entirely on the law."

Teck found this odd. Something deep in him said that this was significant, but he couldn't pinpoint what it was. He decided to think about it later.

"Did they," he asked, "did they select another man?"

"They voted for Fantidaimi, but the lord also refused. He said he was a merchant, not a soldier, and too old anyway."

"Then what happened?"

"The meeting broke up in confusion."

"Anything else?"

"Yes, fompus. The families are moving women and children to Ciarra, Porcus, other islands. There are virtually no chopters left out there."

"And the men?"

"Most are staying here."

Teck nodded to the clerk in dismissal, then turned to the visiphone. Lord Cullu still sat there, in the same slouched position; he appeared comfortable in the transparent inflatochair. It crossed Teck's mind that Cullu was due to come by again, full of inquiries.

"Huroka."

"Good news, fompus. We've got nearly all of the new recruits assembled. Four hundred are now camping on West Beach, and the last hundred are airborne at this point."

It pleased Teck to hear an upbeat note at last. Huroka's side of the operation had gone smoothly from the start. All Tower Fompa had been cooperative. The logistics had worked without a hitch. The men were here.

Teck calculated quickly. Four hundred men of the occupation, nearly two hundred Castle reserves, five hundred recruits. He'd have the power—a thousand men against the disorganized Senate. He felt better. Even without the men of Gash he was superior.

He made a note to call Rhumus and to give him command over the West Beach troops. They'd be useful in mob control. I'll master that rabble yet, he thought, suddenly euphoric.

Lord Cullu rose from his chair in a hiss of air. Teck welcomed him mentally. He'd have something to tell the Deep One.

"You've done a splendid job of organization," he said to Huroka. He felt more like a commander again. "Keep it up."

"How's it going?" Lord Cullu asked.

"Splendidly," said Teck. He beamed at the lord through sparkling, rimless glasses. "A few mishaps here and there, but on the whole the plan is unfolding as I knew it would."

Penta Mart felt himself carried by the stream of people. They were all around him in the dark, marching in silence, men, women, adolescents, oldsters. The ascent was steep and stole the breath away. He knew that they'd be walking in silence for that reason alone. Now there was an added motive. Up ahead he saw the lights. He estimated twenty to thirty tundrati up there. They blocked the highest, narrowest part of the pass.

The column stopped. Penta was not at the head of the column but a little ways back. Nevertheless he knew what went on up ahead. Young men would be climbing the steep rock face on either side. They'd be barefooted; rolls of rope would hang over their necks; they'd have steel hooks over their shoulders. They'd throw the ropes down from the top. Other young men would move up on those ropes, quickly, arm over arm.

He was glad he had come to see this operation. Not that there was much to see in the darkness. But he sensed the people around him, the real revolution. The revolution is breathing all around me, he thought, breathing through thousands of people in one breath. The air was damp and cold. The aromatic odor of

Nary pines was everywhere; it mingled with the musk of forest ground.

He had moved about all night restlessly. He had been far to the south and had seen the people marching on dusty roads between endless flats of *lacrema veni* blooms covered by light wire mesh. He had been down on West Beach and had mingled with the recruits. Then back to the Fairgrounds. There he had wandered from fire to fire and had listened to the people. The visit also gave him a chance to observe the Contorti operation from close up and to collect intelligence from the Fangani. He had listened to Leo, had heartily endorsed his plan. It fit in well with the overall scheme.

He had roved about, but he had kept in touch with his lieutenants by radio.

He looked down on himself, wondering if his clothes were visible in the dark. He was dressed like a lac farmer: loose, baggy white pants tied at the ankle; leather patched over the knees; sandles; an armless, collarless white shirt.

Next to him, catching "her" breath was his "wife"—a muscular Cushman with a bulldog face got up like a peasant woman. "She" carried two baskets (the radio and the power pack), and under the kerchief tied around "her" head were earphones.

To get here they had caught a ride in a lac van. A few were still moving. On the way they had passed the tundratus parties sent to block the passes.

The tundrati had made good time. Penta wondered if these soldiers sensed the masses of waiting people below them, wondered if they heard the faint clicking of hooks as they grabbed the rock face.

Soon the people surged forward again, Penta with them.

His radio man came close and whispered: "The leader reports he's arrived at the pass, is moving forward."

"Tell him, 'Cushman's Luck.'" The leader didn't know that Penta was here. Penta didn't want to interfere; his official presence would disrupt the operation. The leader would feel the need to check every decision.

A ripple of talk began up ahead and rolled back past Penta. The silence rule had been lifted or, more likely, the leader had ordered the people to talk. The tundrati mustn't be surprised. In their anxiety they might charge or call in reserves.

Penta picked up the pace and moved closer to the front, slightly amused at the huff and puff of his "wife." Tono was a good man. The radio and power pack were heavy. Penta hurried; he wanted to see the action from a better vantage point.

The tundrati heard the mob. Bright beams of light fell on the people. The shadows were harsh. Accustomed to darkness, the people blinked, shaded their eyes. But they kept moving.

"Halt, turn about. This pass is blocked."

The crackling, amplified voice came from somewhere behind the light.

"Halt. We will shoot."

The people moved on. The leader had a good eye. Precisely one hundred meters from the light he stopped the column, just outside the range of light-weight beamers.

The tundrati were less perceptive. They filled the road with beam fire, a wild criss-cross of crackling light lines, sparkles.

Throughout the halted crowd young men moved

forward. They were armed with knives, sticks, and large, flat, spatulated lacmordos.

For perhaps three minutes Penta observed nothing except the erratic, futile shooting of the soldiers and the forward filtration of the young men. Then the rock bombardment began from above, a heavy crashing and rumbling. One rock demolished the power pack that fed the floodlights. They went out slowly, turned orange, then died. There were screams, yells. Some of the beams turned upward, others were cut off.

As the young men charged in the darkness on naked feet, Penta ran forward with them. Tono grunted behind him. Random beams caught, cut down some of the youngsters. But casualties were light, and the battle was over almost before it began.

Penta arrived at the site a little behind the attack. He heard a radio crackling.

"Ferri eight, Ferri eight, come in Ferri eight, this is Rhumus one."

The call was repeated once, then again.

At last someone lit a torch. In its flickering flame a young man found the radio, crouched down next to it, and answered.

"This is Ferri eight."

"Ferri eight, give us a report."

"They've turned about. We shot twenty, thirty of them, and now they're on their way down again."

"Good work, Ferri eight. But for God's sake answer your radio."

"Will do, Rhumus one."

Penta saw that the young men were already helping tundrati out of their uniforms. The people had caught up and were moving through the pass, cheerfully chattering.

Tono came up again, whispered: "Guess what?"

"The leader reports the pass has been taken, they're moving down into South Bosom."

"How'd you guess?"

"I'm psychic. Tell him: 'Good show.'"

21 — THE PEOPLE

At 0500 on Octo 16 (Octo 23, System reckoning), around 350,000 people (equivalent to 23% of Faltara's population) were deployed on the site, each 100 led by a cadre. The display had two objectives: (1) to demonstrate Contortus inability to prevent mass movements of population and (2) to demonstrate to the Senate that Balto enjoyed overwhelming popular support. The Senate–isolated from the people, inexperienced in mass politics, relying on narrow palace intrigue, and overawed by the trappings of Contortus power (torch cannon, troops)–chose to disregard the signal with consequences described below.

> *—Ronald Frederick, Report to the 23rd Subplenum of the Centennial Party Central Committee*

People, people, people. Like a strong wind testing the countryside in preparation for a storm, their voices and sounds murmured, coughed, whistled and hummed. The sound had awakened Jan long before dawn, and he had listened to it lying in his hammock in a tent pungent from the smoke of a hundred fires.

Now it was well past noon, but that rushing and roaring of massed humanity had not diminished. If anything it had grown louder; that single voice had

213

taken on an edge; the people buzzed angrily now like a nest of honey-furs stirred by a stick.

Jan enjoyed an excellent view of everything. He had climbed a giant ponok tree not far from the roofed-over stand where the Senate would sit and lounged comfortably on a lower branch. The stand was to his right, the jousting field and all the people to his left.

Just look at them, he thought. Just look at all those people!

Torn clouds raced across the sky, and sunlight intensified and faded in moving patches illuminating hundreds of colorful tents topped by flapping family pennants. The people occupied virtually all open space. They sat on the jousting field, filled the narrow alleys between complexes of tents, and overflowed beyond the tents to cluster thickly on a slope beyond tent city. They formed a carpet of many colors over the nearby land—a carpet woven of Faltara's folk.

Jan hoped that all these innocents would survive the day. Not far from the ponok tree on which he perched, tundrati had set up four torch guns facing the crowd some minutes ago. The tall men of Ignazio's bodyguard manned these eight-barrelled weapons. Late the night before Penta Mart had visited the Fangano tents to explain his strategy; Mart had said nothing about these awesome instruments of death.

Jan knew how these so-called "dragons" worked. Once, long ago, he had seen a film of the dragons at Potsla Run; it had been shown by the Castle-lords as part of an evening's entertainment. Each barrel of each gun could cut a swath through the crowd assembled here, a swath five hundred meters long and fifty meters wide. The chemical flame would leave in its wake charred, black, smoking stumps of men. Jan wondered if Mart knew about the dragons and their destructive power.

A transport saucer far to the north broke through the sound barrier and sent back a dull report. The levitron industry went on working despite the events here in the south.

Taking that boom for a signal, the crowd broke into an impatient chant. "Se-nate, Se-nate, Se-nate," they chanted. The chant grew in volume as more and more people picked it up; then it subsided again only to grow stronger later.

The Senate's box to Jan's right hand was empty. The senators were meeting in a nearby tent—trying to decide how they should act, Jan guessed. They had been conferring all through the night, unable to make up their collective mind. The sudden appearance of the dragons had delayed them yet more.

The people chanted, "Se-nate, Se-nate." Jan shivered with tension. He wanted to be done with this. He longed for normal life again; he longed to be with Sophie on the porch of her parent's home in the foothills of Crasnus—just holding hands and talking about nothing much at all.

Then at last Jan saw motion. Tall, thin, ancient Fantidaimi came at the head of a column of senators and entered the senate's stand from the rear. Derisive cheering arose from the crowd when the people sighted the senate. The metallic noise of banged pots and pans came to Jan's ears. He turned to see the Fangano tents.

Balto had been told about the Senate's arrival. He emerged from among the tents and walked toward the Senate's stand dressed in grey overalls and heavy boots, just like a commoner, not like a lord, but the people saw him and broke into a ragged cheer. Then thousands of voices took up the "Bal-to, Bal-to, Bal-to" chant.

Balto felt as if he were a ship moving over an ocean of people. They clapped and yelled; hands reached out to touch him, he saw faces, faces, faces—old, young, smiling, yelling faces. He shook some of the most insistently proffered hands and tried to smile and look a lot more confident than he felt. The torch guns up ahead worried him; Mart had said nothing about the guns, and the tundrati arranged behind him were absolutely loyal servants of Ignazio Contortus.

At last he reached the edge of the crowd. He moved boldly toward the cannons, passed between two of them, and took up a position in front of the Senate's box.

Neither Fantidaimi nor the other senators looked at him, but their faces and postures communicated a decision nonetheless. After a night and half of a day of debating, the Senate had decided to back the Contorti. The guns had been persuasive in the end.

For a moment Balto felt an icy chill, a doubt, and he recalled moments of danger on icy mountain slopes back home on Felicitas where one wrong step could set off a deadly avalanche. Then he pushed aside all doubts.

"Lords of the Senate," he called—and started. Magnified by loudspeakers, his voice was flung out over the crowd behind him. The surprise and displeasure he saw on the senator's faces told him that the speakers had been placed by Penta Mart's agents during the night. Why? To tell the Senate that someone else had charge of these events? To let the people hear the senators' decision?

"Lords of the Senate," Balto called again. "I am

here by appointment with you. I claim victory over Ignazio Contortus and thus I claim his duties, powers, and responsibilities. Ignazio is dead, and all of you saw him die."

"Wrong! Ignazio Contortus is alive. The claim is challenged."

Now Solumnos Teck emerged from behind a line of tundrati that extended from the Senate's stand all the way to the Contortus tents. He strode forward, smiling, a confident figure in a silver robe, his dark hair pasted down flat on either side of a severely straight part.

High up in his tree perch, Jan had expected some such move by the Contorti, but he had expected an outcry by the crowd as well. Surprisingly, no outcry came. The people stood silently. Then Jan saw the reason why.

Masses of red tundratus jackets had appeared on all sides behind the people. The soldiers were moving forward, through the crowd, and made Jan think of liquids mixing—the red tundratus liquid mingled with the whitish-brownish liquid of the people of Faltara. The liquids then separated again. The tundrati took up formations in front of the Senate's stand, the guns to their back. They made a solid body of a thousand men, each armed with a beamer. Despite himself, Jan had to concede that the maneuver had been extremely effective.

Meanwhile, a small squad of tundrati, tightly bunched around some object in their center, had emerged from the complex of Contortus tents and marched toward the Senate. Teck had turned and watched the squad as it approached. The soldiers stopped before the Senate, separated, and then revealed Ignazio Contortus lying on a stretcher. To show that he was really alive, Ignazio waved feebly toward the Senate with a pudgy hand. His body was covered with bandages, and his face was cast in a grimmace of pain.

Solumnos Teck now surveyed the senators, his rimless glasses sparkling. He felt uplifted by a sense of power. Here he stood—where he had planned to stand. He had brought it off. Even the crowd was now under his thumb thanks to those beautiful dragons at his back. The new recruits had been brought to the Fairgrounds from Fenari during the night, but Teck had assigned their operation to the most responsive men he would find—Ignazio's bodyguard. This undercover leader of Cush, he thought, with a sideways glance at Balto, will have his true reward. The dragon ate mobs and was the perfect neutralizer. Teck chose his words and spoke.

"Lord of the Senate," he said, "I have good news for you. Contortus is alive although not very well. But as a special gesture of respect for you, my lords, he has consented to appear before you. He has survived the vicious challenge of this renegade lord and demands rejection of the Fangano claim. You may not know this, but gentlemen, the Lord Balto is a member of Cush."

"My lords, I am amazed," Balto rumbled in immediate reply. "You saw Ignazio die out there. You saw him pierced several times in the early rounds. You saw him ride back with a lance-head in his guts. You saw me pierce him through both lungs. You saw him fall. You saw his blood gush out like a river, and you saw him shudder when he died. I looked into his dead eyes on the ground and they were glazed over. And now he is here. If you believe that, lords, you are a bunch of cowardly fools."

"Lord Balto," said Fantidaimi, "this is Ignazio Contortus, and he is clearly alive."

"If this is Ignazio, then I must have fought another

man. And, if I fought another man, Ignazio forfeits the match.''

Teck did not like the big man's confident air and aggressive tone. It was inconsistent with the presence of four dragons and a thousand troops. He thought it time to remind this fool, and those imbeciles of the Senate, that Solumnos Teck held all the cards around here. He controlled the Contortus household, and thus the tundrati, and thus the planet of Fillippi.

''Fantidaimi,'' he said, omitting to say ''lord,'' ''my lord Ignazio has been severely wounded and he tires easily. I have gone out of my way to follow protocol, but enough is enough. I won't listen to the ravings of this ryant-ox. I demand immediate, unanimous rejection of this claim.''

''And I demand to see Ignazio's wounds.''

Balto's words resounded loudly over the crowd, and when the people understood him, they raised a cheer that grew into a mighty demonstration of sound. Slowly the cheering died away.

Teck glanced uneasily at the people. They should be meeker back there, he thought. They face flaming death. Then he dismissed the thought.

''The mob is restless,'' he cried with flip unconcern. ''They don't know the power of these cannons. Lords—your decision.''

''Senators,'' Balto cried, ''you will see his wounds even if I have to undress him myself.''

Several things now happened in quick succession. Balto smashed a fist into Teck's face, and Teck fell to the ground. Nearby tundrati moved forward to assist the fompus, but crackling beams of power cut them down; they tumbled to the ground. Balto had reached the stretcher by this time. He grabbed Ignazio by folds of tunic and lifted him off his convalescent couch. He pulled the pudgy lord across the turf, feet dragging, and stopped with his limp cargo immediately before the senators.

A look of terror had spread over Ignazio's fat face, and so great was his fear that he allowed himself to hang from Balto's hand. Balto slapped the lord across the face. "Stand up you fool," he cried. Ignazio stiffened his sagging legs. Then Balto reached inside the neck of Ignazio's tunic and with a powerful motion he ripped the garment open and tore off the bandages. Ignazio stood before the Senate naked to the waist, a pitifully flabby figure. His skin shivered with goosebumps, but he showed not the slightest scratch. The crowd went wild with cheering.

Teck heard that sound from his position on the ground. He had risen to his hands and knees and searched the grass with a flattened hand for the glasses Balto's blow had dislodged. Impotent fury tore Teck's innards. He could not understand why Balto had not been stopped. Then he found his glasses, put them on, spat out some blood, and rose.

"Tundratiiii," he cried. Rage and excitement turned his voice into a shriek. "Fiiiire! Attaaaack!"

The crowd fell silent for the fraction of a second. Then it roared its anger with a single voice and began to surge forward.

Jan observed that initial surge from the branch of his ponok tree. He saw isolated groups of men and women in the midst of the crowd, people who tried to stop the slowly gathering stampede. But the few Cushmen amidst the masses lost control over the people. The people came like a tidal wave, and as they came they turned into a mob.

Teck stared at the scene in astonishment. The color had drained from his face. That solid block of soldiers,

a thousand men in bright tundratus jackets, stood un-
moving. They had disobeyed. Some few of them lay on
the turf in twisted positions, and Teck saw that they
were palace guards. Ignazio's personal bodyguards
tried to fire the torch cannon; the men were moving
frantically, hammering at the triggers, exchanging car-
tridges, but the guns refused to fire.

Unspeakable rage gripped Teck. "Tundratiiii," he
shrieked again; he did not know what else to do and
refused to believe his eyes. "Fiiiire," he cried. "Attaaaack." Then he saw the mob. It seemed to be a
single person—its face distorted by passion, its mouth
wide open with shouts. Teck let out a little cry of terror
and turned. His feet became entangled in his long silver
robe as he tried to run away; he fell to the ground and
never got up again. Thousands of feet trampled over
him and crushed his body into the soil of Faltara.

Jan watched the carnage from his ponok tree. The
tundrati in formation threw off their uniforms. Beneath
those jackets they wore ordinary clothing and green
armbands to identify them as operatives of Cush. They
tried to take command over the people, but the people
had become a single, mindless, murderous person. It
killed, slashed, trampled, and burned. It tore down
tents and set them on fire. It leveled the camp. It
slaughtered lords, fompa, slaves, women, children. As
evening fell it drifted away, loaded with loot and heavy
with shame.

At the end only one complex of tents stood on the
Fairgrounds of Faltara. It was the Fangano complex.
Above it flew the green pennant of the platypus.

22 — AN EXCHANGE OF TREASONS

The Lord Fangano felt the ever-so-slight motion of Dominus as the city rode the waves off the shore of Faltara. The stormy season had come at last, and giant waves moved across Fillippi's measureless oceans under a steel-gray sky. The wind blew at gale force. Huge Dominus, so motionless upon the waters as a rule, trembled a little under the battering of waves.

The city had been brought down from the sky soon after Cush's victory; the precious levitron that had held it aloft had been shipped to the refineries for export. "We have to sell every liter of lac we can produce," Balto had told the revolutionary council. "We have to move this planet into the modern age."

Balto was the provisional president at present. He had authority to deal with System, to negotiate a new lac deal, and to organize elections. He had been the natural choice. Not only had he defeated the Contorti; but Penta Mart had disappeared. He had dropped from sight the day the mob had killed off the concession. Search parties still combed the area for the leader of Cush.

They searched in vain. Penta Mart was alive and well—but only Balto knew that. Penta Mart was alive and well. And at this moment he prepared to take his departure from Fillippi.

Balto watched the preparations from a balcony of the Contortus palace. In a hidden courtyard below him stood a flat, circular spaceship of the type called Scout V. Penta Mart had just entered the craft after a final wave to Balto, and now the craft was beginning to shimmer and glow as Mart activated its photon engines for the slow atmospheric departure.

"Must you leave?" Balto had asked the revolutionary during a secret farewell dinner the night before. "You are a hero now and Fillippi has become your home. Back home you will be tried for serving Commercial System, and you might end up in prison again. Here you can be the father of a planet, live in honor and comfort, and die with your name securely inscribed in history."

Mart had sighed, hearing those words. Staring at the green shimmer of his upheld glass filled with cicillo, he pondered a reply.

"I have to leave," he said at last, "and for more reasons than one. I am a man of Empire, and I am committed to that way of life. I would never feel at home in your culture—too much individualism. Now that the mission is accomplished, I must return to my own kind. And you have made it easy for me to do so, Balto. If I bring the Commissars a Scout Ship V, they may forgive my little treason."

"One treason deserves another," Balto said. "You have done a service to Commercial System, and Hondo Thackus owes you a little favor for all those years of work. He is not very likely to pay up, so I guess I will do it for him. But what about the people of Fillippi? Don't you think you owe them something? They need your leadership."

Mart chuckled. "We have a saying back in Empire," he said. "'People need heroes, but the best heroes are dead.' Another saying is, 'to secure harmony, burn the heroes' writings.' I burned all my papers just before the joust, and soon I will be a dead hero—exactly what Fillippi needs. I guess I have lived among you System people long enough to have become something of an individualist myself. I want to be remembered as a legend, a man who died at the zenith of his career, the man who gave freedom to Fillippi. Meantime my duty calls.''

Down in the courtyard, an envelope of light had surrounded the scout ship. It rose slowly into the air, high above Dominus. Balto looked up at the ship and saw it wobble three times in a last gesture of farewell. Then the saucer turned on edge and zoomed away like a luminous wheel, a fire discus. In seconds it passed into the clouds.

''May you walk in the path of the Great Serendiptiy.'' Balto murmured; he was repeating Mart's parting words. Then he turned toward the north, his eyes on the clouds.

He waited about twenty minutes. Then he saw five saucers breaking through the clouds—a large one escorted by scouts. The large ship carried Commercial System's embassy come to negotiate.

He turned into the palace to receive Crudo Gridabulous, System's special emissary.

EPILOGUE

It was the grandest wedding ever celebrated on Potsla Run. The entire world came to watch the festivities—all the tafchukos from Faltara and from the other islands as well, all members of the Tesso cult, and hundreds of the curious.

Tents had been erected all around the extensive estate to house the people. Those prominent among them occupied the guest houses where only lords had stayed in years gone by. The President slept in the mansion cared for by none other than Sondus Rigg himself.

The occasion lasted for three days, a symbolic number—the number of a tafpa's humps, as the tafchukos said; of the three virtues, as the tessori asserted; of the peaks of Crasnus, as the people liked to think.

The folk at Potsla roasted a herd of ryant bulls each day to feed the hungry. Jugglers juggled, musicians played, young men walked on stilts, the people danced. The tafchukos drank cicillo, the tessori sipped lac tea, the people guzzled beer.

On the second day tafchukos from the Run staged an re-enactment of the Faltara joust. Shy Fillip gave a superb performance as Ignazio Contortus and was the darling of the day.

The wedding took place on the third and last day, in the evening. She wore the white gown of the musician with a golden belt around her slender waist; her blond hair had been raised into a bun and secured by a red ribbon to mark her as a leader of the revolution. He wore tafchuko clothing—a ruffled white shirt with a hero's red sash running from shoulder to waist, blue britches, and black boots.

They were both exceedingly shy and self-conscious—more frightened in the festive, glittering setting under candles and puffing balsam burners than ever amidst the worst dangers of the Siege of Faltara.

The President gave the first toast that night. He saw this as a symbolic wedding, the convergence of the very best on Fillippi: the ardent, impulsive, sacrificial tafchuko tradition and the cool, controlled, and transcendental legacy of Tesso—united now in that which embraces and dissolves all differences: love.

The toasts went on, the festival continued. Music. Dancing. Indoors and out.

But when night deepened the two slipped away, aided by friends. They drove off in a small floater festooned with garlands and ribbons.

FRITZ LEIBER

ISAAC ASIMOV

There are a lot more where this one came from!